S0-BNY-988

You, Me and He

You, Me and He

Brooke Green

Full Circle Publishing

Full Circle Publishing

P.O. Box 16868
Philadelphia, PA 19142

Copyright ©2008 Brooke Green
Published by Full Circle Publishing

Layout and Book Design: AMV Publishing Services
Cover Design: Marion Designs
Book Packaging: Writersandpoets.com

Printed in the United States of America

Publisher's Note:

This is a work of fiction. Names, characters, places, and incidents
either are the product of the author's imagination or are used
fictitiously, and any resemblance to actual persons, living or dead,
events, or locales is entirely coincidental.

All rights reserved. No part of this book may be copied, reproduced,
or used in any way without written permission of the publisher.

Library of Congress Catalog Control Number: Pending

ISBN 10: 978-0-9815340-0-8
ISBN 13: 0-9815340-0-7

First Printing 2008

Acknowledgments

First and foremost, I have to thank God for showing me that He is real and that prayer works.

To my wonderful daughters, Nadira and Gabrielle: everything I do is with you in mind. I love who you are and everything about you. God only knows where I would be if it weren't for you. I want you to always reach beyond your potential and don't let anything or anyone get in your way. Shut 'em down and keep it movin'!! I never thought I was capable of loving anyone as much as I love the two of you. I hope I make you proud.

To my mother, Beverly Peurifoy-Green: thank you for being my biggest cheerleader. Thank you for believing in me and my writing even when everyone else thought it was a joke. Thank you for always having my best interest at heart and showing me the finer things in life. Thank you for always pushing me to do better and to never settle for less than I deserve. After all we've been through, I love knowing that we are now friends. Thanks for the tough love.

To my father, Aaron Green: thank you for always being there and never turning your back on me. Thank you for seeing me through the most trying times of my life, nagging me when I didn't want it and hugging me when I needed it. I'm sorry for all of the gray hair.

To my step-mother: Denise: thank you for making my father happy and being a great friend to me. Thank you for inviting me into your family and dispelling the myth about stepmonsters, (smile).

To my brother and sister-in-law, Sean and Tanya: Thank you for pushing me to do more and build an empire. I don't tell you enough, but I do love you.

To a very special man, George: Thank you for putting up with me, (smile). Thank you for making this book see the light of day. You are a man in every sense of the word and thank you for treating me like a woman. Thank you for pulling me along and putting me in a position to make all of my dreams come true. There is so much I can say, but I'll end it with this, I love you.

To my best friend, EZ Jase: Thank you for constantly pushing me to finish this book. Thank you for being my ride-or-die homie and always having my back. I love you like a fiend loves 3 for 10's. LOL…and thank you Wanda for keeping him in line!!

To my grandparents: thank you for all of the love and support you have shown me.

To my grandmother Helen Robinson-Peurifoy: I wish you were here to hug me one last time. I miss you so much.

Thank you to all of my aunts, uncles, cousins and extended family. Special thanks to Donna for letting me use her name, even though this story is NOT about her, lol.

Special thanks to my cousin Charmaine, my good friends Renee, Debbie, Reggie, Frank, Trip, and everyone else who read the book as I wrote. Your words of encouragement were priceless.

Earl Cox, Thank you for all of your help and advice. You've made this process a whole lot smoother.

Nakea Murray, Thank you for your honesty and help in this crazy book world. Girl you were right, this title is much better!!

To Tish: Please believe that if anybody can do this, you can. Put that pen to paper and write it down! You are a smart, strong and resilient woman. After all you've overcome, you know you have a guardian angel. So make her proud and do the damn thing!!! I love you.

Last but certainly not least, my Jefferson Street Verizon family: Thank you for making me laugh and keeping me on my toes. I wish each and every one of you the very best.

DONNA

Ring!

Damn, not again.

Ring!

I rolled over and looked at the clock: 6:59AM. The phone had been ringing for the last half-hour.

Ring!

Keith must have forgotten to turn the ringer off before he left.

Ring!

I wanted to scream! Normally, staying over Keith's house is peaceful, kind of like having a vacation from my own noisy neighborhood.

Ring! Then nothing. The answering machine must have picked up. Finally.

I sat up in bed and looked around. The bedroom was beautifully decorated, thanks to my flair for color and Keith's wallet. I could not wait for the day when this house would be mine, and I could really make some changes. Compared to my cramped apartment in South Philly, Keith's house in the Wynnfield section of Philadelphia was paradise. Although Keith suggested on several occasions that I move in with him, I had refused. I couldn't have him placing demands on me and taking me for granted *before* the wedding. I knew if I moved in with him, it wouldn't be long before he stopped taking me out to dinner and started expecting me to be Susie Homemaker and cook three meals a day everyday. So instead, I decided to keep my small, stuffy apartment in South Philly and keep Keith wanting more.

"Oh well," I said aloud. "Since my sleep was so rudely interrupted, I guess I'll get my day started."

Ring!

Whoever it is better be dying or damn close, the way they are blowing this phone up.

I snatched the phone off its base before it could ring again. "Hello?"

Nothing.

"Hello!" The caller was breathing lightly into the phone, and I heard voices from what I presumed was a television in the background.

"Um yeah, who is this?" a woman asked with an attitude.

Do I really need this shit at seven o'clock in the morning?

"Excuse me? You called here. Now, who is this?"

"I got your phone number out of my husband's phone, and I want to know why it's in there!"

Husband?

She cut me off before I could respond, "Your phone number has been on my husband's cell phone bill for the last three months, and I want to know why. Don't try that friends shit either," she yelled in my ear, "because friends don't need to talk after midnight!"

"Miss, I think you may have the wrong number," I said, trying not to laugh.

From the sound of things, her man was messing around on her, and now she was on a warpath. I hated to burst her bubble, but she was barking up the wrong tree. I took a deep breath and said a silent prayer of thanks that I wasn't in her shoes. Keith had shit with him, just like any other man, but for the most part he was a good man.

She paused for a moment, and I heard papers shuffling. "I don't have the wrong number," she said before rattling off Keith's phone number. "This is the same number I found on his phone bill and in his phone!" I knew there must have been an explanation, but in that moment I couldn't come up with one.

"Miss, I think you are mistaken. Trust me, I haven't been talking to anyone's husband," I said.

"Look, don't lie…"

"What is his name?" I interrupted her before she could embarrass herself any further, and since she was so sure I was guilty, I decided to humor her and get to the bottom of her accusations.

"Don't act like you don't know, bitch! It's Jarrod!"

Count to ten. This is why I can barely stand women now.

"Understand this, I'm not going to be too many more of

your names. Now, I hate to tell you, but I don't know any Jarrod. So…"

Oh, shit!

"What's his phone number?" Just hearing that name made my heart race with fear. My breathing became short, and I felt the beginnings of an anxiety attack.

"What, are you kidding me?"

"What's the damn phone number?" I asked through gritted teeth.

"2674445982, the same phone number you been calling, bitch! I am so sick and tired of you trifling women who can't find their own man…"

I felt sick. My hands trembled, and my silent prayer of thanks was definitely short-lived.

Forget her! Let her argue with herself, I thought, as I put the phone down and reached over to check the caller ID box.

I scrolled through the last few days worth of calls. Then I saw it: J. James. The most recent one was two nights ago, Thursday at 1:30AM.

I felt sick. I hung the phone up on the still-screaming woman.

Forget her. Now we both have a problem.

I continued to press the "down" arrow on the Caller ID box, which was now becoming my worst enemy. There it was again, Thursday morning at 6:30AM.

Wednesday at 5:46AM.

Wednesday at 12:04AM.

Tuesday at 11:00PM.

Ring!

I began to feel the all-too-familiar knot in my stomach.

"That bastard!" I cursed Keith as the idea of killing him slowly and painfully crossed my mind. I quickly nixed the idea, because I didn't think I could get away with it, and I was too cute to go to jail.

Ring!

"What?!" I screamed into the phone.

"Don't get tough, now, ho! Now, I want to know how long you've been messing with my husband!"

"I am not messing with your husband," I said numbly.

"Don't lie. Come to think of it, do you even know which one he is? I mean, how many men are you screwing with your trifling ass?"

"Probably not as many as your husband," I said through the lump in my throat.

"Excuse me?"

I cleared my throat, time to get real. "Miss, I hate to tell you, but it's not me Jarrod is fucking," I choked.

"Don't lie to me…"

"Listen!" I cried. "It's not me, your husband has been fucking my fiancé." *Again.*

I sat on the phone listening to Jarrod's wife scream obscenities at me. I knew the feeling, because I was once in her shoes. I knew she didn't believe me, because who would want to believe the man they are supposed to spend the rest of their life with has a thing for other men?

"Miss, can you please calm down and listen?"

"Calm down?" she yelled. "Are you serious? You just told me that my husband is fucking a man, and you want me to calm down?"

"Yes. Look, this is not even my house. The number you called is my fiancé's, Keith. I don't live here."

She inhaled sharply. "Keith? Keith who?" I could tell the name struck a chord of recognition by the way she asked the question.

"Keith Reed. He and Jarrod were roommates in…"

"I know exactly who Keith is and how they know each other," she spat. "We went to school together. He and Jarrod were roommates, and, as a matter of fact, Keith introduced the two of us." She sighed as though all was well. *Ha!*

"We haven't seen each other in years," she continued. "I had no idea they had even gotten back in touch with each other…Hold up!" The idiot just remembered the bombshell I'd dropped. "Are you trying to tell me Jarrod and Keith are fuckin'? You have lost your damn mind! My husband ain't no faggot, bitch! I got a good mind to call Keith myself and tell him the shit you just said." Then, almost to herself, "I don't believe this shit."

Enough was enough. It was time to make her a believer. "Maybe he's not a faggot, but I do know for certain he likes dick, so I guess that makes him something doesn't it? So, if he ain't gay, I guess he's about to be, 'cause he's sure enough getting practice! If you don't want to believe it, then fuck it, but just know this, I saw them together! Yup, that's right. I saw your precious husband with my man's dick in his mouth. Why would I lie about some shit like that, huh? Why do you think they lost contact in the first place?

It wasn't by accident, but because I made it happen! So whether or not you believe it, I don't give a fuck! Fuck what you think, and fuck your cock-sucking husband!" The tears I had been holding back now flowed freely down my face.

She stayed on the phone, breathing heavily, and then I heard a low moan that turned into a loud wail. Then she hung up. I sat with the phone to my ear until the aggravating tone used to alert you of the phone being off the hook broke the silence. My silent cries turned to sobbing, complete with choking, heaving, and gagging. I ran to the bathroom just in time to empty the remnants of last night's steak dinner into the toilet. I heaved and cried for about ten minutes, until my head pounded. I peeled of my nightgown, which was now wet with tears and God knew what else, and turned on the shower. I climbed into the warm shower and stood under the water while thinking about how I wound up in this situation. How many women know their man is bisexual and choose to stay? I don't mean, "suspect them." I mean, "know," as in, "caught in the act."

I know I'm not the only one, so where in the hell are the support groups? I thought.

*   *   *

The day that I discovered Keith's double life started off perfectly. I worked as a receptionist/secretary at a small law office in Drexel Hill, and, normally, I dreaded going to work on any day, much less Mondays. But on that particular day, I was in such a good mood that I thought nothing could

*spoil it. My boss was in court that morning and would be out
of the office for the rest of the day, so I was able to finish my
work without interruption. By twelve o'clock I found myself
anxious to get out of there, so I played sick and had one of
the office clerks fill in for me. I left work in a hurry with one
thing on my mind: my man. Since it was his first day off in a
month, I figured I would treat Keith to an afternoon of good
food and great sex. Keith ran a property management company with his father. Over the last few months, the business
had been especially demanding, and I had convinced him to
take a well-deserved day off. The night before, we lounged
around and had long, lazy sex. I shivered as I remembered
Keith's skillful tongue. I have yet to meet another man who
could do the things he could with foreplay. On the way to
Keith's house, I stopped by our favorite seafood spot and
picked up two shrimp and scallop platters. I dialed his number on my cell, but hung up before he answered, opting instead to surprise him. When I arrived at his house, I parked in
the driveway and unlocked the front door with the key he'd
recently given me. His house was still quiet, except for the TV
in what sounded like the family room. I emptied the platters
on the new china we picked out together, and as an afterthought decided to strip my clothes off right where I stood. I
then tiptoed down the hall to the love of my life, hoping the
sounds of the television would disguise my footsteps. I laughed
to myself when I heard the sounds of pleasure coming from
the TV. Keith and I often enjoyed watching porn together, the*

kinkier the better. The thought of what was to come had me dripping wet with anticipation.

I threw the open the door and yelled, "Surprise!"

"Surprise" was the understatement of the year. The few seconds it took for my mind to absorb what I was witnessing felt like a lifetime. The only sounds to be heard were the plates falling to the floor and Jarrod getting that last swallow of Keith's seed.

"Oh hell, no!" I screamed. "Ain't this about a bitch!"

"Donna...I..." stuttered Keith. He jumped up and shoved Jarrod out of his way.

"How in the hell did she get in here?" Jarrod asked. He looked at me as though I were a child who entered their parents' bedroom without knocking first.

While Keith reached for me, Jarrod struggled to get his pants up while muttering under his breath.

"You fucking sissy!" I said as I backed away. I looked over at Jarrod, who was fumbling to pull his zipper up over his rock-hard erection. He caught me staring at his dick and winked.

"Baby, I'm sorry," Keith sighed.

"Don't touch me! You and your bitch in here homo thuggin' like it's ok, and you want me to believe you're sorry?" Out of the corner of my eye, I saw Jarrod staring at me, and it was then I realized that I was still nude. I took Keith's shirt off the chair put it on.

"Yo, you better check your bitch, Keith," Jarrod threatened. I turned to say something to him, but Keith interjected.

"Chill, man, watch your mouth," Keith said. "Get your shit and roll."

"It's like that? It's cool..." Jarrod began.

"Get the fuck out!" Keith and I yelled at the same time.

"Are y'all two bitches seriously in here having a lover's quarrel?" I asked. I looked from one to the other and couldn't help but notice that Jarrod's pants still revealed a huge erection. I turned and ran to the kitchen, trying to find my clothes through my tears.

Keith came behind me, begging me to hear him out. He gathered my clothes that were strewn on the floor and tried to help me dress, but I smacked his hand away and screamed, "Don't touch me!"

Jarrod walked past us and snickered. His erection was still intact.

"Cocksucker!" I yelled right before spitting in his face.

He reared his arm back, and, just as his fist came in my direction, Keith landed a right hook on his jaw.

"Have you lost your fuckin' mind, man? I told you to bounce!" Keith sneered.

Jarrod looked as though he wanted to fight back, but thought better of it once he saw the look of hatred in Keith's eyes. Instead, he walked through the door and, as a final blow, winked at Keith. Before Keith could react, he slammed the door and I heard the sick bastard whistling as he walked down the driveway.

I put on the last of my clothes and headed for the door

without another word. There were plenty of things I could think of to say to Keith, but I knew if I stayed a minute longer there was a strong possibility that Keith would not survive the confrontation. I reached for the doorknob, but Keith blocked my path.

"Move!" I cried as I clawed at his bare chest.

"Baby, please, hear me out. I—"

"You what? You want to talk? Call your man back here and finish talking to him, because you ain't got shit to say to me wit' your freak ass! And if you know like I know, you better get out of my fucking way before I tear this fucking house up!"

"I love you, and I never meant to hurt you..." he began.

"Go fuck yourself, or better yet, go fuck Jarrod!" I spat.

I pushed past him and flung open the door. Before I left, I turned around for one last dig, "I wonder how your father would feel if he heard his son is a flame."

Keith at that very moment could have been the very first black man to turn white.

"My father has nothing to do with this," he croaked.

I smiled at the look of fright that crossed his face. "We'll see."

I slammed the door with as much force as I could muster. I drove home and cried. I cried not only for what I had witnessed between Keith and Jarrod, but also for everything that would never be: the wedding I had been planning, the life that Keith promised me, and even the children he wanted me to carry. Thirty minutes later, I walked through my front door and collapsed on the couch. My home phone was ringing nonstop. Keith would not give up. I turned my cell off in the car after the fifteenth time he called.

I sat on the couch, not wanting to believe this was happening to me. Did I miss some signs? Keith was in no way effeminate, nor did he exhibit any signs of gay behavior. It was almost second nature to me to assume a man had homosexual tendencies, so when I met Keith, I paid close attention to his behavior. I thought he was perfect in every way. Guess I was fooled. Normally, I thought I could spot a "down low" brother a mile away, and my girlfriends would challenge me while we were out bar-hopping. We would sit at the bar facing the door and pick apart every man who walked through the door. My best friend Sabrina was once engaged to a cop named Lance, who all but had a flashing neon sign screaming "ASS LICKER" on his back. She met him one night while we were out, and he was one of the men I dubbed as being gay. He walked over to us and tried to kick some tired game to me, and when I literally laughed in his face, he turned his attention to a willing Sabrina. They had been dating for several months when Lance proposed and Sabrina happily accepted against my warnings. She was so sprung over the freaky things she would tell me they did together, she refused to see him for what he really was. Our friendship was almost destroyed when I sat her down and brought my suspicions to her attention. She refused to speak with me about Lance and my suspicions, and even went so far as to threaten me if I continued to bring it up. Sabrina finally saw the truth when, on the night of Lance's bachelor party, she thought it would be a good idea to surprise the guys at the hotel with an impromptu strip tease. Knowing this would turn Lance on tremendously, she was giddy with excitement as she told me of her plan. She dragged me and her two sisters, Leah and Tanya, to the Residence Inn at the Philadelphia Airport where the bachelor party was being held. We finally located the room by following the loud music and the parade of about five fine brothers exiting an H2 Hummer. We snuck around the pool to the patio of the ground floor studio, and with our ears to the door, we listened to the whoops and hollers coming from the group of rowdy men.

I grabbed Sabrina's arm before she could knock. "You know, this might not be a good idea. I mean, what if you walk in on something you don't want to see?"

"Girl, please. You talking about some nasty dancers? Hmph, trust me, once he gets a taste of what I can do, he won't think twice about those birds." She laughed at her own humor.

Leah, the youngest of the three sisters, laughed, "Plus, Lance has some fine-ass friends, and I ain't had none in a minute, so I'm about due."

"Yeah, but just because he might like a strip tease behind closed doors doesn't mean he wants his homies to see what you're working with. He might not take too kindly to that," I reasoned.

"Whatever. You can stay out here if you want to, but I'm going in," Sabrina said.

"Come on, girl, you know once she sets her simple-ass mind to something, you can't stop her," Tanya, the oldest and most sensible of the three, sighed.

"Okay, I'll go, but don't say I didn't warn you," I said, all the while knowing that some drama was about to pop off.

Sabrina tapped on the patio door, but because the music was so loud no one inside heard her knocking. After the second knock, she decided to peek through the curtain, which was partially open.

"What the fuck!" she screamed with a look of horror.

"Told you," I muttered under my breath.

"What is it? Let me see," Leah said as she scrambled to get a look.

Before I knew what was happening, Sabrina reached around us, grabbed a patio chair, and smashed in the entire windowpane of the door, causing the curtain to fall. What we saw before us was nothing like I had imagined. I was prepared to see some exotic dancers performing various sex acts with each other and probably even the groom-to-be himself. But lo and behold, there was Lance in a chair, stripped down to his black silk boxers with his hands on the ass of the man giving him a lap dance.

"Oh shit," Leah said with her hand over her mouth, trying to conceal her growing laughter.

When I looked around the room, I saw that the five

brothers we saw on the way in were the exotic dancers hired to entertain the guys.

    Sabrina reached Lance in a matter of seconds and attacked him like a rabid dog, biting, kicking, and scratching him. The man giving him the lap dance jumped out of the way just in time, but he still caught a shoe in the back of the head, courtesy of Leah. When his partners in crime tried to pull Leah off of him, Tanya whipped out her pepper spray.

    Then pandemonium.

    Lance pushed Sabrina to the floor. Why did he do that? Sabrina reached in her purse and pulled out the .38 revolver she carried for times such as those. Everybody in the room scrambled to get away from Sabrina's trembling trigger finger, not to mention Tanya's toxic pepper spray.

    "Sabrina!" I screamed as I grabbed her arm.

    BAM!

    The gun went off, everyone hit the deck, and Lance slumped to the floor.

    "You killed him!" Tanya cried hysterically.

    Lance lay there moaning and pleading for his life.

    "Sabrina, please, let's get out of here. He's not worth it," I begged. I looked around the room and suddenly felt like a victim. We were in a hotel room, surrounded by a bunch of cops who had basically been pulled out of the closet. Not only did we know their dirty little secret, Sabrina had just shot one of their fellow officers. I was frightened for my life. Shit, she only had five more rounds, and there were at least twenty

guys in the room. If they got that gun away from her, we were as good as dead.

"No, that pussy is still breathing, and I can't have that. It's not fair!" she cried, "How could you?"

Tanya and I wrestled the gun from her hand and shuffled her out of there.

As we were leaving, I turned and saw Lance struggling to get up. "What a waste," I said to them all.

After it was all said and done, Sabrina's freedom was spared. Lance, who was only grazed by the bullet, decided to play dumb when questioned about the shooing and gave a bogus story about a robbery. Since he was a cop, he figured it would be in his best interest to keep the real story quiet. He knew that if he pressed charges, Sabrina would squeal like a pig and his reputation, as well as those of his co-workers, would be destroyed.

Years later, we laughed when Sabrina told us that when she would ride him she would play with his balls, and he would always seem to raise his ass just enough for her fingers to rub his asshole. She thought nothing of it until after the incident at the hotel.

"I thought he was just trying to give me the long stroke," she would laugh.

As I remembered Sabrina's disastrous relationship, I sat there wondering how I wound up in damn near the same situation. How could I have known something was up with Lance, but not with Keith? I thought about Keith. He was indeed a very handsome man, and at 6'2" 225lbs, dark brown with baby-soft skin, he was just my type. And the fact that he had money to burn certainly raised his attractiveness quotient. I began packing the few things Keith kept at my place. I looked at his boxers to see if there were any stains that shouldn't be there.

"What in the hell am I doing," I said to myself, "sitting here looking at some underwear?"

I sat down and cried once again, and the longer I cried the angrier I became.

"I should get my little cousin, Snoop, to fuck him up," I said aloud. "Yeah, that'll work. That shit would be right up his alley, or, better yet, I could just ask Sabrina to shoot him. I bet she'd get a kick out of that!" I shook the thought out of my head. "Damn, I really don't want him hurt. Besides, I don't want to have to explain to anyone why. Knowing my nosy-ass family, they would love to hear that my knight in shining armor has been knocked off his high horse."

I got up and walked the short walk from my small living room/dining room/kitchenette to my bathroom. I stripped down and stepped in the shower, hoping to scrub away the memory of what I'd just witnessed. The warm shower water lasted about seven minutes, then turned ice-cold. "Why'd he have to go and fuck it up? I shouldn't have to live like this!" I shrieked while trying to escape the frigid water.

After drying off, I studied myself in the full-length mirror. I had always felt confident up against other women. Shit, look at me: 5'5,"and a tight body that could rival Halle Berry in her best red carpet moment. Shoulder-length hair, all mine, and a face that was a nice cross between Gabrielle Union and Nia Long. I have never had a reason to feel insecure standing next to another woman; it's all eyes on me. Thoughts of Keith and Jarrod invaded my thoughts, and, no matter how hard I tried, I couldn't shake the memory. Eventually my mind wandered to Jarrod's perfect body and even better erection. The sad part was if I had met Jarrod first, I would have gone after him. He was about 6'4," and had a milk chocolate complexion with hazel eyes. And, to top it off, he had a bald head. When Keith introduced the two of us, I instinctively knew he was a dog. On occasion, Keith and Jarrod would hang out and I would nearly drive myself insane thinking of the two of them on the prowl for other women. But who knew there was no need to worry about Keith falling for another woman? Ha! I should have been worried about his homies…My God! His homies! "Homos" is more like it. All of those late night fight parties. Yeah, fight parties my ass — sword fighting, maybe. So much for happily ever after.

*   *   *

Ring!

I sat up with a jolt. "Shit," I said. "I must have fallen asleep after I got out of the shower. I was supposed to be packing my shit so I can escape this twisted situation as quickly as possible."

Ring!

"Yes!" I snatched the phone off the receiver without looking at the caller ID.

"Damn, baby," Keith laughed. "I'm sorry if I woke you. I

tried your cell, but I didn't get you. Everything okay? You sound upset."

"You tell me. You forgot to turn the ringer off and…"

"Oh man! I'm sorry, Donna. But I figured I would leave it on so I could wake you. Remember, you said you didn't want to sleep late, because you have to go to Sabrina to get your hair done?"

Everything happens for a reason.

"Oh yeah, I remember. By the way, I've been meaning to ask you something. Have you heard from Jarrod lately?"

He paused and then asked, "What made you ask me that?"

"Just answer the damn question!"

"Yeah, I ran into him a couple of months ago at the Black Men's Empowerment League's Networking Symposium. Why do you ask?"

"I ask because I just got off the phone after having to explain to his wife that it wasn't me having pillow talk in the wee hours of the morning with Jarrod for the last three months."

"His wife? Jackie?"

"Yeah, you son-of-a-bitch, his angry-ass wife! Now, can you explain why I had to do that?"

"It's not how it seems. Jarrod…"

"Pardon me? I don't think I heard you correctly. What's not how it seems? The fact that I literally caught you with your pants down, with a man no less, and he has suddenly reappeared? Oh, I see. Maybe it's the fact that you have been creeping behind my back with Jarrod again. Or is it that you conveniently forgot the promise you made to me?"

"Donna, please. I have not forgotten anything. I promised you then and I promise you now, I am not contacting Jarrod. After the symposium, he began calling me at the office. Soon after that he must have gotten my number from one of the committee members, because he started calling the house. In the beginning, he was only inquiring about buying some commercial buildings. I referred him to a few of my other contacts, but he started getting persistent. Baby, yes, he has been calling me, but I swear to you on everything I love that I have stopped taking his calls. I didn't mention it to you because I thought he would go away."

"Well, he hasn't, and I made sure his wife knows the truth. Your story sounds good, but to tell you the truth, I really don't know what to believe at this point, Keith."

Keith sighed deeply.

"Hold on," I said. The tears had returned full force. I put the phone down until I was able to regain some of my composure. I refused to show Keith any kind of emotional vulnerability.

"I'm back," I said after picking the phone back up.

"Are you okay?"

"Why do you care? You weren't thinking about my feelings when you were creeping."

"How could you say that?"

"Easy. Just as easy as you could sneak around and be deceitful." My head was pounding, and I was tired of the conversation. "Look, I have to go, and I'm tired of being lied to. We have nothing to talk about anymore, Keith. Call Jarrod. I'm sure he'll be happy to hear from you." With that, I hung up the phone before he could respond.

The phone instantly started ringing, but I ignored it. I looked around his bedroom and considered trashing it. My mind flashed to Angela Bassett in *Waiting To Exhale* as she exacted her revenge against her cheating husband, and I smiled. There were several thousand dollars worth of artwork that I knew he would surely miss if I destroyed it. My mood began to lift as I opened the door to his closet and fingered his thousand dollar suits and shoes. I couldn't decide whether to burn them or shred them. Either way, I knew the look on his face would be priceless at the sight of the damage, and I considered waiting around just to see it. I wanted him to feel some pain. I wanted to hurt him, and I figured the best way would be to hurt him in his wallet. The phone, which had been ringing nonstop, interrupted my daydream and brought me back to my senses. Reality set in as I thought about his insurance. I knew that he was well insured, and he would have all of this shit replaced in the blink of an eye. The last thing I wanted was for him to come out on top. I pictured him laughing at my expense and spending the insurance money on another woman, or even worse, Jarrod. I shook my head, trying to erase the thought. The phone continued to ring and I answered it mid-ring.

"What, Keith? What do you want?"

"Donna, hear me out," he sounded out of breath. "Have I done anything in the last two years to give you any reason to believe I am being anything but faithful to you?"

"No, but…"

"Listen, I understand how you might have reservations, and that's my fault because I wasn't honest about myself in the beginning. But I have done everything in my power to make you feel secure. Just know that I love you more than I love myself, and Jarrod is not going to be a problem."

"How can you be so sure?"

"I'll change all of my numbers if I have to."

"Yeah, but we went through all of this before, and look what happened. He still managed to worm his was back in."

"You are absolutely right, but how he got my number this time was out of my control, Donna. Tell you what, I'll change them again, and I'll be sure to let the committee members know that if anyone needs to contact me to take their number and I will call them. How does that sound?"

"Okay, you do that, and we'll see what happens. And Keith, don't make me regret this." But I already regretted giving in so soon, because I knew I was letting him off too easy. I couldn't shake the thought of another woman standing in my place and reaping the rewards of being Keith's woman. I wanted to believe him, because I wanted to be his wife, and I knew he would provide me with a life I could not otherwise afford to provide for myself. I knew I was being selfish, but he owed me for even staying with him after learning of his sexuality.

He breathed a sigh of relief. "Well, what did Jackie have to say?"

"Who? Oh, she was saying I was fucking her husband and what not. But she damned near had a heart attack when I told her what was really going on."

Keith sighed once again, but this time it was filled with tension.

When I decided to remain in the relationship, I promised

Keith and myself I would not let that side of him be known to any one else. He didn't think his reputation could withstand people knowing about his bisexuality. I agreed. After all, not many people would understand me staying with a man I caught receiving a blowjob from his best friend.

"Did you really have to tell her?" he asked.

"Are you serious? Why wouldn't I tell her? Shit, I wish somebody had put me down. And why should I protect Jarrod? He obviously didn't give a fuck about me when he was doing my job!" I was getting angry all over again. "She deserves to know."

"Okay, okay, I don't want to argue. You're right. But I hope she'll be okay. Jarrod mentioned she is pregnant with their first child, and she has wanted kids for as long as I've known her."

"So sad, too bad." I could not care less about her or her feelings. I had my own to deal with.

"Well, back to you and me. Are we still on for your birthday? I've got something special planned for us."

"We sure are, just as long as you promise it'll be good," I said, happy to be talking about the prospect of my birthday gifts. "I can't believe I'm turning thirty." I groaned loudly. "Will you still love me when I'm old?" I laughed.

"You'll always be twenty-nine to me."

"Thank you, baby." I wondered if he said the same thing to Jarrod.

"Have a good day. I love you. Oh, I almost forgot, I left my platinum card on the dining room table like you asked."

Now that's what I'm talking about.

"What would I do without you? I love you too!" Once again, all was well in Paradise. But for how long?

After we hung up, I unpacked my things and made the bed.

Maybe I'll move in after all; I need to keep a closer eye on things, I thought.

Ring!

"Hello?" I said, happy again.

"Um, hello? This is Jackie, Jarrod's wife." I rolled my eyes and wished I had checked the caller ID before I answered.

"Yes?"

She hesitated and then asked, "What you said to me earlier, were you serious?"

"As a heart attack."

"I…" She began crying, "It's just that I don't really believe that, but I feel like I need to hear you out."

"Listen, I apologize for being so blunt earlier, but I was just as hurt and angry as you. I've been where you are right now, so trust me, I understand."

"Do you think we can talk more? I mean can I meet you some place? Today?"

She sounded like a scared little girl, and I began to feel sorry for her.

"Well, I have an appointment at 11:00 so I could do it around 2:30."

"That's fine. How about we meet at TGIF in Cherry Hill at 3:30?"

"Sounds good."

"Okay, I'll be waiting at the bar."

Isn't she pregnant?

"How will I know you?"

"I'll be wearing a red coat."

"See you then."

"Bye."

All of this shit and it isn't even 9:30. What a day!

KEITH

Damn, damn, damn!

After I hung up, I got up from my desk and paced the length of my office. I couldn't stop thinking about the conversation with Donna. The walls started closing in on me, and I felt an anxiety attack coming on. I gathered my belongings and rushed out of the office. I headed to my father's office to tell him I was finished for the day and, if necessary, I would be available on my cell phone. As I turned the corner, I saw him standing at the door to his office, pawing Mrs. Knickson, our Office Manager, who is also the wife of our real estate broker, James.

My father, the man's man and a real stand-up guy.

I watched for a few seconds, until I began to feel like a Peeping Tom. In an attempt to escape undetected, I tripped over a trashcan that was behind me.

Just my luck.

"Oh! Hello, Keith," Mrs. Knickson said, her already pink face turning crimson.

My father, on the other hand, thought nothing of it, although he did seem a little agitated because I had interrupted his own real-life soft porn.

"Son, I didn't see you there. Come in, there is something I need to discuss with you." He turned his attention to Mrs. Knickson's retreating ass. "Thank you for the estimates, Nadine."

"Anytime, Mr. Reed. Just doing my job."

I wonder what kind of bonus she gets for that, I thought.

I followed my father into his office and closed the door. I sat down in the chair facing his desk, waiting.

He cleared his throat, "How's it going?"

"Could be better." I looked at my watch as a hint for him to get to the point.

"Good, how is your little friend, what's her name…Diane?" I wished I could smack the smirk off of his face.

"It's Donna, and she's great, thank you. As a matter a fact, you should be getting your invitation to the wedding in the next few months. We've decided on the Bahamas." It was my turn to smile as he absorbed my last statement. My father made no secret of the fact that he loathed Donna. In his opinion, she was beneath me, and I was making a mistake by taking her seriously.

He grunted, "Yeah, well, Dr. Harper and his wife have invited us to dinner next Saturday night to celebrate Celeste's law school graduation. There is only room for the two of us, so you are going to have to do without your friend for one night." He looked at the calendar on his desk. "Oh, and on Sunday afternoon, First Day Baptist is having a Men's Day Luncheon for the league members, and I expect you to be there. No excuses this time."

Is he for real? I thought. *He actually has the nerve to*

play self-righteous, when he knows he is the reason I avoid those church functions in the first place. I caught the pastor's wife giving him a blowjob in the port-a-potty at last year's annual church picnic.

"Well, I hate to disappoint you, but Donna's birthday is next weekend, and I have already planned our Saturday evening. But I will try to make it on Sunday."

"Keith, I'm sure you can celebrate her birthday another day. How about Friday? It's still the weekend."

"Dad, stop trying to run my life, I'm a big boy." He held a look of contempt on his face as I held his stare. Years ago, I would have been the first to break the stare out of respect and even a little fear. But now, I refused to give him the satisfaction.

"That's just it, I trying to help you become a man. But to do that, you need a real woman behind you. Now, that girl you have now is a nice piece of ass, but she is not someone who can fit into our world. Celeste, on the other hand, is a classy lady who is going places."

"So I guess being a man means being like you?" I asked.

He smiled. "Look at you, fawning over a gold digging hoodrat with no future. I remember how you fell apart when she left you. It was a disgrace. You barely made it in to work! And what happened when *she* decided to take *you* back? You went running. You could have any woman you want, but you choose to scrape the bottom of the barrel. You *play* with girls like her, not marry them."

"All right, Dad, but answer this, what's the measure of a man, huh? Is it trying to screw every woman you can, with no regard for her feelings? And for the record, Donna is more than enough woman for me. Not like the girls you run around with. Thank God for Mom, because while you were out screwing the town, she was teaching me how to be a man. Yes, I was devastated when Donna and I broke up, but I know a good thing when I have it. So yeah, I went running back, you damned right, because as a *man* I can admit when I'm wrong. So if you'll excuse me, I need to go, I have to go see my *woman!"* I got up and walked to the door, then decided to go in for the kill, "Oh, and by the way, Pop, you might want to spray. I can still smell *Mrs. Knickson's* scent." He jolted forward in his chair and flexed his fists as though he wanted to fight.

Fuck you. I wish you would, I thought. The look on my face must have betrayed my thoughts, because my father relaxed in his chair and, without looking at me, dismissed me with a wave of his hand.

I left the office and walked past a still-blushing Mrs. Knickson. "Don't work too hard, now. Tell Mr. Knickson I'll be in touch."

Her voice caught in her throat as she answered, "Bye, Keith."

I walked out of the building and was hit by the chilly March air. Tugging my coat tighter, I jogged to my new Range Rover and hopped in. While the truck heated up, I thought about the trouble Jarrod had become once again. I had to admit, running into Jarrod at the symposium was bittersweet, a mixture of anger and lust. When he began calling, it was like two buddies catching up on old times. Then the conversation began to turn sexual, and Jarrod began pushing the issue of getting together. I had never been necessarily been attracted to Jarrod, but he was sexy in a rogue sort of way. He had a cockiness about himself that made you want to tempt fate. I almost gave in to temptation, because I had not been with a man since I had been with Donna, but I intended to keep my promise to her. I hated having to lie to Donna about the content of our conversations, but she would not have understood. Not many women would stand by their man after finding him in such a compromising situation. But she would certainly not stand for a repeat performance. After all of the work I put in to get her back, I would not ruin it, not for Jarrod or anyone else, for that matter.

*   *   *

After finding me with Jarrod, it took about two weeks for Donna to finally answer my calls. She would answer and curse me out, but at least she was picking up, and that was a start. I even took up standing near her car as she exited from her job as a receptionist for a law firm. But when I was almost run down in her attempt to escape my pleadings for forgiveness, I tried other methods. I began sending dozens and dozens of red, yellow, and pink roses to her job, and I felt like I was making progress because she didn't refuse them. But I stopped that once I received a phone call from the lawyer she worked for threatening legal action for stalking and harassment. I was all out of tricks when I came up with a brilliant idea. I went to the King of Prussia Mall and stalked every jewelry store for the perfect gift.

We had been dating for a little over a year when I proposed on Christmas Eve. Donna was ecstatic, but she had some reservations about the ring.

"Baby," she cooed, "I don't mean to be ungrateful, but this isn't exactly the style of ring I wanted."

Here we go, I thought to myself.

She had begun leaving little conspicuous hints around, like placing advertisements for diamond solitaires in platinum settings in my briefcase.

"What do you mean? This is a 3.5 karat solitaire, and, look, it's set in platinum," I countered.

"True, but the ring I wanted was round cut and *this* is emerald cut. See?" She gestured to her adorned finger. "This doesn't catch the light quite like a round diamond." She smiled that devious smile that always made my stomach turn.

We had only been engaged for about twelve minutes, and she'd already managed to make me regret proposing. I had to restrain myself from snatching the ring off of her finger and calling the whole engagement off. I always knew that Donna, like most of the women I met, had gold digging tendencies. But this was crazy. I took her hand in mine and looked at the ring again. The ring cost more than she made in six months.

"You don't like it?" I let her hand fall.

"Of course, it's the thought that counts. But next time you buy jewelry for me, I think I should tag along." She said it like I had bought her the wrong shade of panty hose.

She gave me a half-assed kiss before jumping up and running into my kitchen to call her chickenhead friends, no doubt.

I never gave her complaint a second thought until our relationship was at stake. I was sure that buying a ring was the only thing I could do to get her to at least open the door. I left the mall with a month's salary in a black velvet box. By the time I arrived at Donna's street, it was getting dark outside, and I tried to find a parking space that was reasonably close to her second-floor apartment. I double-checked the alarm on my truck and walked to her building. Because of the amount of crime and despair, her street and neighborhood in general really left a lot to be desired. It was certainly not a safe place, especially for a single woman, which is why I wanted her to move in with me. The entry door to her building was partially open and when I walked in I was face–to–face with Dante, Donna's neighbor, and two guys who looked to be in their late teens.

The bigger of the two teenagers reached in his waist and said, "What the fuck you want?"

I put my hands up and took a step back but Dante calmed the boy down. "Chill, man." Then he turned to me. "What's up?"

I attempted to shake his hand, but decided against it once I saw the sandwich bag filled with what I assumed to be drugs. Instead I just nodded my head in greeting and climbed the stairs to Donna's apartment. I listened at the door for sounds of life on the inside. When I heard the television, I knocked softly.

"Yes?" Donna asked from somewhere inside the tiny apartment.

"Baby, it's me," I called.

"Baby? Negro, please! Jarrod lives in New Jersey, remember? Now, get the fuck from in front of my door before I get those dudes out front to beat your ass and take your precious truck!" I prayed that Dante and his two flunkies weren't listening.

"Donna, can you please just let me see your face? I promise, if after today you really want nothing else to do with me, I'll leave you alone." I pushed my ear to the door.

"Bitch, please. Step!"

"Fine, but I have something for you, and I would rather not leave it out here. So could you open the door and get it, and I'll be on my way?"

She sucked her teeth and flung open the door. I extended the hand that held the box. She looked as though she wanted to smile but thought better of it. Instead, she snatched the box and slammed the door in my face. I put my ear to the door to hear her reaction. I knew it was my last chance. I was all out of tricks.

She must have been standing on the other side of the door, because I heard a quick yelp.

"Goodbye, Donna." I called through the door.

I heard her fumbling with the doorknob, "Keith, wait."

When she opened the door we were face-to-face and she held out her arms.

"Yes?" I asked sheepishly.

"I forgot to give you your key."

It took me a moment to comprehend, because I wasn't sure I heard her correctly.

"Oh, and thank you for the ring. It's beautiful," she continued.

"Just like you. You are very welcome," I said as I slid the key from her outstretch palm.

My shoulders sagged as I turned and made my way to the steps.

"Keith," she called out.

I looked over my shoulder at the woman who was indeed the love of my life.

"Would you like to come in?"

"Please." I nearly jumped for joy at the sound of those words.

She held the door open for me to enter. I sat down on the sofa and waited.

She stood over top of me with her hands on her hips. "Okay, so talk. You've chased me for the last month, and now I'm giving you a chance, so talk."

"I've missed you, baby…"

"First of all, cut the 'baby' shit. I stopped being baby when you let another man suck your dick."

"Okay. Donna, let me start by telling you how sorry I am…"

"You got that right. You are the sorriest man I know," she cut in.

"Jarrod and I were roommates in college, and that's where it began." I paused to take a deep breath. I knew I would have to explain myself, but that didn't make it any easier. I had never told anyone what I was about to tell her.

"I'm listening, for now. Go ahead."

"Well, I'd been insecure about my sexuality for years before I had even met Jarrod. I knew that I was attracted to men, and that scared me. I didn't think of myself as gay or even bisexual, because I thought gay men were flamboyant, talked with a lisp, and swished when they walked. It was real hard, because you know what kind of person my father is, plenty of women to spare.

"For a while, I tried to live up to his reputation by sleeping with as many girls as I could. I think knowing that I still found girls sexy and attractive may have been the only thing that kept me sane.

"I did not have any encounters with men until I went to college and met Jarrod. We didn't become roommates until sophomore year, and we hit it off immediately. He was like the brother I always wanted. One night after we came in from a late night of drinking, I stripped down and got in bed. I remember feeling someone get in my bed, but I was too tired to pay it too much attention. I don't know how much time passed before I realized what was happening. I opened my eyes and saw someone sucking me off and, I have to admit, it felt good. I closed my eyes and thought Jarrod must have invited a couple of people over. But who? Our dorm room had become a popular hangout spot on campus, so it wasn't unusual for people to be in and out at all times of the night. I opened my eyes and tried to focus in the dark. Then I saw exactly who it was. Jarrod. I tried to move him off of me, but he refused and I was on the verge of cumming. I think it was the thought that another man was giving me head that put me over the top. When he finished, he looked at me with a satisfied smirk, then got up and went to his bed. I turned over to face the wall, not believing what had just happened. I couldn't believe it. A part of me was excited, while another part was disgusted. I was very confused, because, like me, Jarrod was something of a ladies man. Even after I introduced him to Jackie, he always had a revolving door of women willing to do anything he wanted. He had money and good looks. I guess we were cut from the same cloth, except Jarrod seemed to get a sick pleasure out of treating women badly." I stopped to take a breath. I never thought I would need to tell the story to anyone.

"I need to apologize to you again," I said. "I am very sorry, because I was wrong and I know I hurt you."

"Yes, Keith, you did hurt me, and I don't know if I can just forgive and forget," she stopped and looked at her ring. "How many men have you been with?"

"None while I was with you." She cut me short with a look. "Well, except for what you saw with Jarrod, and only one other person."

She couldn't seem to take her eyes off the ring. She had placed the original engagement ring on her right hand and held both hands out to admire her fingers.

"Please, just give me a chance to make it right. If you give me a chance, I will spend the rest of my life making it up to you."

"I don't know, Keith. The thought of you kissing someone else, especially a man, freaks me out. I don't even want to think about you getting fucked or sucking a dick..."

I sat back in shock. "Donna, I swear on my mother's grave, my lips have never touched another man's lips or dick. And I have never, ever been penetrated."

She looked doubtful. "What about condoms? How do I know you don't have AIDS?"

"Any time I have sex I use condoms. You know that."

"I certainly don't remember seeing a condom while he was sucking your dick."

"We can get tested together if you like." I had no reservations about getting tested, because I was sure I was clean.

"I don't know about you, but I'm getting tested anyway." She rolled her eyes. "So, have you and Jarrod been fucking all this time?"

"No, it was only the time I told you about and the time you caught us together."

"So if I had not walked in, what would have happened?"

"Nothing else, I promise."

"How can I be so sure this won't happen again, Keith? I mean, it's one thing to compete with a woman for your affection, but how in the hell can I compete with a man? Because there will be no anal sex jumping off. This ass is exit only."

"You don't have to compete with anyone, baby, I mean, Donna. I want you and only you. What happened with me and Jarrod will not happen again."

"Well, how did it happen in the first place? How does a man just wind up sucking your dick, Keith? Tell me that."

"I won't sit here and blame it on anything but a moment of weakness. I was weak."

"Yeah, well, if you were weak once, you'll be weak again. I don't want to worry about the next time you and Jarrod have a 'boys night' if you and he are fucking doggy style on the floor. My aunt always told me, the first time you fall for something you're a victim, and every time after that you're a volunteer."

"I'll tell you what, I will cease all communication with Jarrod and hand over his account to my father. I will change my phone numbers, whatever you want me to do."

She eyed the ring again. "We'll see. But I will let you make it up to me. I need a favor."

"Name it."

"My mother got another eviction notice and she has to have the money by close of business Monday. I hate to ask you, but if she gets evicted, then she and my brother will have to move in here, and I can't have that. She only needs $1200, and I really don't have it."

"No problem, baby." She didn't correct me, so I continued. "You know, you could always move in my place. I mean, it will be your house too once we get married, and you've already put your own personal touches on it."

"No, I'll pass. We will have plenty of time to play house after the wedding. You think you could write a check out now? I'm going over there for dinner."

"Sure." I wrote the check to cash and handed it over. "Baby, you didn't give me a chance to give you your new ring properly. Can I see it for a minute?"

She took it off and looked at it with the same adoring look she used to use on me.

I got down on one knee, "Donna, I love you more than life itself. You complete me, and I feel alive when I am with you. Would you do me the honor of accepting my proposal, again?"

She never took her eyes off the ring. "Yes, Keith. I accept."

I placed the ring on her finger and kissed her hand.

"I hope no one else knows about this, Keith. I wouldn't be able to take it if everyone knew your dirty little secret. It would be very embarrassing."

"Don't worry about that. I would never tell anyone. It's a part of myself that I've struggled with my entire life." I chuckled. "My father would probably disown me if he knew."

"Probably."

*　　*　　*

After that night, Donna refused to sleep with me for over three months. She made sure we were both tested for diseases twice before she even let me kiss her. Everything was in perfect order until Jarrod came back. It was probably for the best that Donna found out when she did about Jarrod calling me, because I felt myself almost ready to give in. Donna hit the nail on the head when she said she could not compete with a man. While I can appreciate a beautiful woman, men possess a certain raw energy and fiery passion that women just don't have. Even the smell of a man gets me excited. Don't get me wrong, I have been with all different types of women, some who were into things that freaked even me out. I once had a woman ask me to join her and her boyfriend, who was also bisexual, in a three-way. I declined the offer, because that's not my style.

Jarrod had begun wearing me down after about a month's worth of phone calls, and I was just about ready to give in when he started speaking badly about Donna.

He told me, "I can't believe you are going to marry that ho. And for you to throw our friendship away over her, man, that's foul."

I refused to take his calls up until a week ago, when he apologized. "My bad, man. It's just that we've been friends for a long time, and it fucked me up when just like that it was done."

He started talking about old times, and again we were just like two old college buddies.

Donna

I headed over the Ben Franklin Bridge to Cherry Hill after Sabrina finished relaxing my hair and talking my ear off with the latest gossip. She would do her gossip like Wendy Williams would do her Blind Items.

"What hoodrat from 46th and Brown was seen coming out of the abortion clinic on 38th St. with her mother's new husband?" she would ask.

The person she would be referring to would almost always be in the shop, and ten minutes later, in true Wendy Williams form, she would get a "Tourettes moment" and scream out the offender's name. The woman would jump up and run out of the shop, and everybody in the shop would crack up laughing.

I told Sabrina, "One day somebody is going to kick your ass for that."

"Hmph, I wish a bitch would jump. I got something for that ass." she would pat her purse, which held her gun. "Ain't my fault people doing foul shit. Somebody should kick their ass for doing the shit they do." I could only shake my head at her and her logic.

I made it to TGIF at 3:15. I checked myself in the mirror

and, as usual, Sabrina put her thing down because my hair was tossed. I locked the car up and walked into the restaurant looking for a woman wearing a red coat. I spotted her sitting at the bar nursing a drink, pregnant as the day is long.

My god, that poor child, I thought. *It's bad enough its father is a homo, but its mother is going to give it Fetal Alcohol Syndrome.*

I walked up to her. "Jackie?"

She turned to face me. "Yes? You must be Keith's fiancée. I'm sorry I don't know your name."

"It's Donna." I looked at her drink.

"Oh, it's only ginger ale. No drinking for me until my bundle of joy arrives." She rubbed her stomach and managed a smile. "Sit down, please. Our table should be ready in a few."

I sat next to her at looked at her belly. She was huge. "When are you due?" I asked in an attempt to break the ice.

She immediately brightened up. "In three weeks, and I am very excited. This is our first child."

"Congratulations. Keith said you always wanted children. Do you plan on having more?" Big mistake. Her eyes welled with tears, and she looked to the floor.

"Not if what you said is true."

"Oh, it's true all right."

"I'm sorry for calling you all of those names. It's just that I've known for a while that Jarrod ran around on me, but ever since I announced I was pregnant, he's gotten worse. Almost flaunting his affairs in my face. Now this comes up, and I feel like my world is really falling apart." Before I could respond, her name was called and we made our way over to our seats. I took that moment to check her out. Jackie was as pretty as pretty gets. She stood about 5'8" and was the color of coffee with thick black hair that hung to the middle of her back. Even pregnant she was in good shape.

We sat and ordered drinks. When the waitress departed, the inquisition began. "Can you tell me about Jarrod and Keith?"

As I recounted what I saw as well as what Keith revealed to me, her emotions ran the gamut. She looked shocked, angry, sad, and sometimes damn near hysterical. A few times, she even gagged.

"I don't fucking believe this. Jarrod would be the last person I would suspect. And Keith, he was always such a sweetheart. A gentleman, even." She began to sob.

"I know exactly how you feel. I was in your shoes once. Hell, I'm in them now."

"How could you stay with him, knowing that?"

"Well, the way I figure, Keith is everything I want in a man. I know he loves me, and he takes care of me in all the ways a man should. And another thing, with all of this down-low stuff going on out here, with him there's no guessing. I know what he is, and I accept it. But he knows that I will not stand for him cheating on me with a man or woman."

"I guess you have a point, but you only know because you caught him, not because he was upfront, right?"

The way she was questioning me made me feel defensive, because I didn't like having to defend my actions to a stranger. I wasn't sure if she was being condescending or not, so I searched her face for a sign. Once I was sure that she was sincere, I answered her question.

"Yes, and he knows he was wrong. But with this out in the open, we keep it honest."

"Honest is one thing Jarrod is not. I don't know what I should do. I quit my job after I found out I was pregnant, and now Jarrod controls all of our finances. He uses it against me too. He wants me to account for all of my spending down to the groceries. I know we're not broke. Shit, he's up for partner next year at his law firm. But he's a bastard about giving me money. He practically gives me an allowance every month, and if I need extra money, he turns it into a federal case. He tries to hide bank statements from me, saying that it's none of my business, because it's not my money. I even have to bring receipts back when I purchase things for me or the baby. Donna, the list goes on and on, so I know that if I left him, he would make it hard for me."

"He's the one cheating, so why should you leave? Correct me if I'm wrong, but doesn't the wife get to stay in the house? Plus, you're pregnant so you can't leave."

"I know you're right, and I'll consider it, but first I have to find a way to ask him. He can be a little scary at times, especially when he gets angry.

"That's what 911 is for. You better get with the program."

She opened her mouth to say something, but stopped as the waitress returned to check on us. When the waitress left, she leaned in close and said, "Do you think Keith and Jarrod are still sleeping together? I mean they were on the phone at all times of the morning and night."

"I did ask Keith after you and I spoke, and he says nothing is going on. I can't be sure if I believe him a hundred percent, but I plan on keeping my eyes and ears open. So, what are you going to do about Jarrod?"

"You want to know something? I'm not even sure I want to ask him. I'm in denial. Like, if he doesn't confirm it, then it's not really true. Weird, right?" She managed a weak smile.

"No, I see where you're coming from. But you can't keep your head in the sand forever, you know." I held back a smile because, after all, misery loves company, and I felt good knowing I wasn't the only person in my situation.

"I don't think I can handle this right now. My biggest concern right now is having a healthy baby." Jackie laid her hand on her belly, and her wedding bands nearly blinded me. I snuck an inconspicuous peek at my own ring, which, compared to Jackie's, was less than adequate. I slid my hand under the table and contemplated asking Keith for an upgrade.

We sat through lunch and continued talking. Jackie was actually very nice, a nice change from Sabrina and her mess. After lunch, I walked Jackie to her SUV, a brand new Yukon Denali. I took out a business card with the name of the lawyer I worked for and wrote my numbers on the back.

"It was nice meeting you. Call me if you just need to talk, and call *him*," I said, pointing to the lawyer's name on the business card, "if you decide to divorce."

She took the card and hugged me tight, "Thank you so much. I'll let you know what happens."

Since I was in the area, I decided to head over to the

Cherry Hill Mall to purchase an outfit and a few early birthday presents for myself. Armed with Keith's Platinum Card, I had the time of my life. I figured he owed me for all of the drama.

Thank God for a man with good credit, I thought while driving home.

JACKIE
AND
JARROD

Jackie took the long way home to give herself sometime to think. She wasn't sure if she could believe everything Donna told her. Besides, a man who loved women as much as Jarrod couldn't possibly be gay. Maybe Donna was wrong, she thought, but just in case she wasn't, Jackie decided to keep her eyes open for anything unusual before she confronted him.

*   *   *

Jarrod was certainly not the best husband to Jackie, but he'd given her the life she'd always wanted. Jarrod came from a wealthy family in which both of his parents were lawyers. After the fifth try, Jarrod finally passed the New Jersey Bar and struggled to find a firm. His mother called in a few favors, and he was invited to join a fairly successful firm in Northern New Jersey. After a few years, Jarrod proved himself to be an exceptional estate lawyer and was now being considered for a partnership within the firm.

Jarrod and Jackie were college sweethearts who made plans to get married almost immediately after Jarrod passed the Bar. Jackie was in heaven. That is, until Jarrod revealed his true colors.

When speaking of she and Jarrod's relationship, Jackie began to measure time in relation to the wedding. Everything became either before the wedding or after the wedding. Before the wedding, Jarrod impressed Jackie with his charming personality and the fact that he would go out of his way to make her feel special. When Jarrod proposed marriage, Jackie could not be happier. She had visions of the proverbial big suburban house with a white picket fence. She imagined herself and Jarrod cooking romantic dinners together, taking long vacations, and eventually having at least three children. However, after the wedding Jarrod began to exhibit the signs of being a selfish, self-centered, and, at times, manipulative person. It did not take long for Jarrod to begin coming home later and later, and sometimes not at all. He would accuse Jackie of not being a good wife because she still held a job. But she refused to leave her job as a customer service manager at Verizon. Working gave Jackie a certain amount of independence that Jarrod did not like. He thought women should hold a more subservient role in the relationship. He had made it known to her on more than one occasion that his ideal wife would be barefoot, pregnant, and ready to tend to his every need. Jackie felt as though Jarrod was not the man she fell in love with. When they were in college, she loved the fact that she and Jarrod shared the same values and ideas of how a relationship should work. Jarrod was also her biggest cheerleader when she earned a promotion at work after only a year of working there, which is why she could not understand his sudden change in attitude.

Jackie would often turn to Ms. James, Jarrod's mother, to seek out advice about her situation. Ms. James explained to Jackie that Jarrod had always blamed her for his father walking out on the family. He felt that if his mother had stayed home and tended to her husband's needs, then he would have stayed.

Ms. James told Jackie, "Jarrod is a lot like his father, very controlling and insecure. You just make sure you always have your independence. Don't ever let him take that away from you. He's my son and I love him, but he leaves a lot to be desired with his views towards women and their roles."

As much as Jackie envisioned herself being a homemaker and stay-at-home mom, she took heed to her mother in law's advice and held on to her job.

All of that changed the moment she discovered she was pregnant. She continued to work until the end of her first trimester, but was soon ordered on bed rest when her blood pressure rose to an unhealthy level. When she broke the news to Jarrod, he seemed happy for the first time in months and went out of his way to be involved with her pregnancy. Up to that point, Jarrod had not taken an active interest in the baby and had gone so far as to tell her that this was "her baby." When she began staying home, he seemed to enjoy the fact that he had a meal waiting for him when he came home. He had even managed to go to a few prenatal visits and become involved in the naming of the baby.

The bliss that Jackie experienced came to a crashing halt the day she showed Jarrod the ultrasound picture. He nearly went through the roof when Jackie excitedly told him they would be having a baby girl.

"Just what I need, another fucking woman in my life," he said just before he walked away.

In her sixth month of pregnancy, Jackie was admitted to the hospital due to extreme high blood pressure. During her five-day stay in the hospital, Jarrod had only managed to visit her two times, and during those times, he'd made sure she knew how upset he was. He would complain about the house being dirty and having to eat takeout. Ms. James visited her several times in an attempt to keep Jackie's sinking spirits up. On her last day in the hospital, Jackie's physician, Dr. Shaw, paid her a visit.

"Jackie, please tell me if this is none of my business," Dr. Shaw sighed, "but is everything okay at home between you and Jarrod? I ask, because when I tried to speak with Jarrod regarding the state of your and the baby's health he was extremely indifferent. He said there are more important things that need his attention."

"Dr. Shaw, I know how it seems, but Jarrod is very busy and we talk everyday," Jackie lied. "Besides, he's busy getting the baby's nursery together. He's very excited."

Dr. Shaw looked like she wanted to say more, but Jackie cut her off, "Thank you for your concern, Doctor. I'll see you in three weeks."

Dr. Shaw nodded her head and turned to walk away. She knew there was more to the story than Jackie dared to reveal, but she couldn't get past Jackie's façade. When she'd spoken to Ms. James the day before, she stressed the importance of Jackie taking it easy to ensure a healthy pregnancy.

When she reached the door, she paused. "You know, Jackie, as your doctor, I can't tell you enough the importance of you keeping your life as stress-free as possible. I remember how happy you were about the baby when I saw you for your first prenatal appointment, and now I cannot help but notice how unhappy you have become. Now, as your friend, I am telling you that if you ever need to talk about anything, I am here for you. You must take care of yourself, and, as a precaution, I want you on complete bed rest until your blood pressure is back to normal or the baby is born, whichever comes first." Dr. Shaw felt bad for having to scold Jackie like a child, but she hated to see Jackie suffer at the hands of her husband's neglect.

Jackie turned her head to hide her tears. "I know you care, and thank you." She cleared her throat. "Well, let me finish getting ready. Jarrod will be here shortly." Dr. Shaw nodded as she shut the door behind her.

Jackie dried her eyes then continued getting dressed. When she heard the knock on the door, Jackie checked her face in the compact, forced a smile, and yelled, "Come in, baby!"

The door opened and, instead of Jarrod, in walked Ms. James.

"Hi, Mom. You didn't have to come today. Jarrod should be here in a minute to take me home. I would have called you when I got home."

"Jarrod called me earlier to ask me to pick you up. He

said he had to go into the office for a few hours. I thought he called you." Ms. James couldn't hide her disgust, because once again her son had left Jackie hanging.

Jackie looked at her cell phone and shook her head, "No, he didn't call. It's Sunday, and he never works on Sunday…" Jackie stopped. "Oh well. I guess if he wants to make partner, he has to go the extra mile, right?" Jackie felt foolish for once again defending Jarrod. She looked away from Ms. James disapproving glare and tried to busy herself with gathering her belongings.

"I'm sorry, Jackie," Ms. James stepped in front of Jackie, forcing her to look her in the eyes. "What my son is doing to you is not right. Now, you can try and make excuses for him, but I know the truth. Don't forget, I was married to a man just like him. I will always love my son, but I don't like the person he has become. He is not a good person, and you can't deny that. What kind of father is he going to be to the baby if he's never around? He needs to be there for you now. My grandbaby's health is in jeopardy because of all of the pressure he has put on you. You have to put your foot down, not only for yourself, but the baby also. You are pregnant, and your health is at risk. Now, that needs to be your number one priority, not Jarrod's dinner." Ms. James sat down next to Jackie and hugged her tight. "Forgive me, but Jarrod's is a grown-ass man, and I raised him to know how to take care of himself. Hell, he should be cooking your meals. Now, I spoke with your doctor, and she said you are to stay on bed rest until further notice, and I will be checking up on you. If Jarrod doesn't like it, he can go straight to hell. I'm sorry, Jackie. The truth hurts, but you need to hear it."

Jackie was now sobbing. Everything Ms. James said was true, and she knew it. The hardest part of all was admitting that her marriage was crumbling right before her eyes. She felt hopeless, but she knew her baby could suffer if she didn't take better care of herself.

She straightened up and smiled a real smile. "You know what, Mom? You are absolutely right. So if you don't mind, I would like to get out of here. I need to get home and have a talk with Jarrod."

When Jackie arrived home, there was no sign that Jarrod had been home. The mail was spilling from the mailbox and the bed was made. To Jackie and Ms. James both, this was a dead giveaway that Jarrod had not slept there since Jackie had gone into the hospital four days ago. Jarrod never so much as cleaned up after himself, let alone made the bed. Jackie also noticed a few of the suits Jarrod normally wore to work were no longer in the closet.

"Maybe he stayed at the office." Jackie sighed.

"Don't," Ms. James said. "Don't excuse this behavior, Jackie."

After Jackie settled in for a nap, Ms. James went down stairs to wait for Jarrod's arrival.

It was close to 11:00 when Jarrod finally walked through the door. Ms. James greeted him at the door with a look of disgust.

"Have you lost your mind walking through this door at this time of the night? Your wife was in the hospital for the last five days, partly because of you, and you act as though it's no big deal. It's bad enough you barely made it over to see her, but you don't even have the decency to be there to take her home?"

"Please, I am a busy man. I couldn't come to see her every day. Besides, I knew you were there." Jarrod brushed past his mother and casually hung up his coat. When he turned around, he was face-to-face with his mother's scowl.

"Busy? Don't talk to me about busy. Were you also too busy to sleep in your own bed? And for the record, I was there because you weren't."

Jarrod smiled and said, "Thanks for all your help, Mom, but where I sleep is my business."

Jarrod walked to the kitchen with Ms. James on his heels.

"No, it's Jackie's business, and she has run herself into the ground trying to meet your every need while you do nothing but brow beat her and try to tear her down every chance you get. Until that baby gets here you need to make sure Jackie is as comfortable as possible. She has been under a tremendous amount of stress and has been ordered to bed rest for at least the next few weeks."

Her last statement made Jarrod stopped in his tracks and spin around.

"Stress? Stressed about what? She doesn't do anything. I'm the one who goes out and works everyday to pay for all of this." He spread his arms. "And what you call running herself into the ground, I call being a good wife. Well, not all that good, but she's learning by me telling her what I like and don't like. You know, kind of how Dad tried to show you?" He paused for effect and to let his words sink in. Jarrod knew mentioning his father would strike a nerve in his mother, but he could not stand by and let her come into his home and interfere with he and Jackie's relationship. He hated the way his mother always sided with Jackie as though she could do no wrong. "She's not into all of that 'career woman' stuff that caused Dad to leave you. She knows what she has and she is appreciative. So, Mom, let me thank you for bringing her home, but I'm tired, so you can let yourself out. Good night." He turned off the lights and left his mother standing in the dark as he walked up the stairs.

Ms. James could not believe her ears. What Jarrod said hurt, not because it was true, but because she saw just how bad he had become. She felt like arguing with Jarrod was fruitless.

"You need help. Go to hell, Jarrod!" she shouted at his back before slamming the door.

*   *   *

Jackie woke up in time to hear the tail end of the conversation between Jarrod and his mother. When Jarrod entered the bedroom, he ignored Jackie completely and walked over to his closet. Jackie tried to remain calm, but couldn't help feeling hurt and betrayed by his indifference.

"Well, hello to you too, Jarrod. How was work?"

Jarrod remained silent.

"I think we need to have a talk about what's going on between us, Jarrod."

He didn't acknowledge her presence as he undressed and walked into the master bathroom. Jackie watched him until he shut the door in her face. Refusing to be ignored any longer, Jackie walked to the bathroom with the intention of forcing Jarrod to speak to her, but sat back down once she heard the shower running. Jackie knew she would have a fight on her hands if she continued to push the issue, but she knew the survival of her marriage depended on it. She thought of trying to get Jarrod to make love to her, but quickly changed her mind considering he hadn't so much as touched her since she'd announced her pregnancy.

Jackie was more than certain Jarrod wasn't lying in wait for her to deliver, which is why she was not at all surprised he hadn't stayed home this week. She wouldn't be surprised if Jarrod purposely left the bed made to rub it in her face.

She was aware Jarrod occasionally stepped out on her with other women, but he used to maintain a little discretion and respect while doing it. Lately, though, he acted as though she didn't exist. Jackie noticed someone was calling their home and hanging up when she answered. It never seemed to happen when Jarrod answered. His usual late nights began to get later, and eventually he would make his way home very late indeed. And when she'd finally had enough and questioned him about his whereabouts, he stayed away for three days.

*   *   *

Jarrod took his time in the bathroom. He had hoped Jackie would be asleep when he got home, because he didn't want to hear her whining about him not spending enough time at home. Staying away was Jarrod's way of paying Jackie back for not living up to his expectations. He was tired of Jackie acting like his world should revolve around her and her baby. He never wanted children and had no intentions of playing the proud father to a child he didn't ask for. Jarrod used to enjoy being with Jackie and even considered being faithful to her, until she started taking advice from his mother about their marriage. His mother, the bitch, had tried to strip his father of his manhood by dominating him. All his father ever wanted was a wife whose job was to take care of him. But she refused to let him be the king of his castle, finally running him off when Jarrod was a teenager. Jarrod decided at that moment that if he ever got married, he would not tolerate a woman who didn't know her place. He had to admit, Jackie did try to keep a clean house while continuing to work. But when Jarrod told her he didn't think she should work, she said she would rather contribute to the household. This infuriated Jarrod. Deep down, he knew that as long as she worked Jackie would not be totally dependent on him. When Jackie announced she was pregnant, Jarrod was secretly ecstatic, not about having a baby, but because he knew it would be a good time for Jackie to stop working and be the wife he wanted. He knew being the primary breadwinner would guarantee him the upper hand in the relationship. After Jackie was forced to quit her job, Jarrod would come home to hot meals and a smile. But when her doctor and his bitch of a mother started filling her head with all of the nonsense about taking it easy, she expected him to pick up her slack by cooking and cleaning. Jarrod laughed at the idea of doing anything so menial. Instead, he opted to eat out and leave the house in a state of disarray, forcing his mother to come over a few days a week and tidy up.

He couldn't understand the big deal about high blood pressure. People dealt with it every day without slowing down. For the past month, Jarrod had been getting really bad headaches and diarrhea, but he didn't let it slow him down. He planned on visiting a doctor to make sure he didn't have a virus, but he wasn't walking around complaining and acting helpless. He just pushed on, not like his pain-in-the-ass wife. Jarrod thought Jackie was doing the typical woman bullshit, and he wasn't falling for it. In his opinion, the only thing Jackie was consistently good for was sex. She'd even learned to like the rough anal sex he dished out. Although Jackie would always be a willing participant in any sexual requests he would make, Jarrod could not bring himself to arousal with the thought of a baby in the way. What made things worse was that the baby she was carrying is a girl. Jarrod would have been at least a little accepting if it were a boy, but he couldn't bear the thought of another woman running around making demands. And now, the doctor ordered bed rest, just another reason for her to sit around, get fat, and complain. Whatever. Jarrod knew where he could go to be treated like a man, and he planned to go every chance he got. Poor Jackie, she thought she knew so much, always questioning him about other women. Of course, there had always been lots of women, but what would she do if she knew his real passion was men?

He thought, *She wouldn't do anything, because she couldn't. Where could she go? She has no money and no way to support herself.*

And he would make sure she didn't see a dime of his money. So, he planned to continue indulging in the many men he'd met over the years. Tall, short, fat or skinny, he didn't have a preference. Except when it came to Keith. Within the first week of meeting Keith in college, Jarrod knew he had to test the boundaries to see where Keith stood. After he sucked Keith off and he didn't object, Jarrod thought everything from that moment on would be like taking candy from a baby. But when Keith began avoiding him, Jarrod became fixated on having his way with him. The problem was that Keith was never receptive to his advances.

When Jarrod and Keith were in college, Jarrod invited Keith to a privately hosted key party, hoping to loosen him up. The key parties were given at different locations throughout the city and were attended by bisexual men from all walks of life. Jarrod loved the "anything goes" mentality of the parties and looked forward to attending as often as he could. Though sex wasn't mandatory at the parties, Jarrod got in as much as he could, often several men in one evening. Some of the brothers there would simply mingle or even network, which is why he thought Keith would loosen up and enjoy himself, without having the pressure to have sex. Judging from how uptight Keith was ever since he woke up to find Jarrod giving him head, Jarrod had no clue Keith would act on any sexual urges with any of the men at the party. As the party came to an end, Jarrod scanned the room for Keith, praying he didn't leave after discovering the nature of the party. Jarrod saw Keith leaving one of the private rooms and heading his way. He smiled to himself, because he was sure Keith hid out until the end of the party. Jarrod turned livid when he saw Corey, the host of the party, exit from the same back room he'd seen Keith leaving a few minutes before. He couldn't help feeling a little jealous of what he imagined going on in that room. Jarrod's plan was for Keith to get aroused by being surrounded with plenty of men and sex and then seduce him back in their dorm room. But he didn't count on his participating in the festivities. When Jarrod questioned Keith about what went on between him and Corey, he wouldn't admit to anything.

Years later, after graduating law school, Jarrod contacted Keith and once again tried to seduce him, but Keith wasn't having it. Through the grapevine, Jarrod knew Keith kept his relationship going with Corey. The down-low members of The Black Men's Empowerment League, an organization they both belonged to, always spoke about who was with whom, though they remained tight-lipped around those not in "the life."

Jarrod was relieved when Corey moved away, because he knew it wouldn't be long before Keith finally gave in to him. Jarrod waited patiently, knowing as a true down-low man, Keith could only go so long without experiencing the pleasure only a man could give. Then Donna entered the picture. Jarrod hated Donna the minute he met her. He hated Donna because he saw how Keith had fallen for her. She became just another obstacle in the way of his ultimate goal. Jarrod asked around to see if Keith was creeping with anyone else and, to his surprise, Keith seemed to be totally faithful to Donna.

It took about a year before he caught Keith in a moment of weakness, and the best part was Donna catching them in the act. Her walking in on them couldn't have worked any better if he'd planned it himself. Jarrod thought for sure Donna seeing the two of them together would cause her to leave Keith for good. But to Jarrod's dismay, she hung in there. After that incident, at Donna's request, Keith cut off all ties with Jarrod.

For Jarrod, Keith became an obsession. He felt like he had to have him, and he didn't plan to stop trying until he got him. All of Jarrod's life, he'd been able to get anything or anyone he wanted, and Keith would be no exception.

Jarrod had recently decided to attend the Black Men's Empowerment League's Networking Symposium with the hope of running into Keith. Even though Jarrod and Keith joined the league at the same time, Jarrod was only interested in the private parties given by a few of the members. While Keith chose to stay and move up on the committee, eventually being appointed CFO, Jarrod lost interest.

Just as Jarrod thought, Keith was at the symposium, but he was too busy to give him any attention. Jarrod stayed, expecting Keith to eventually greet him, but he had no such luck. A few days later, Jarrod contacted Keith at his office and wasn't surprised that he received a cool reception. Jarrod played it cool, not wanting to scare Keith away once again. He began by asking about investing in real estate, then moved on to reminiscing about their college escapades. He made sure to steer clear of mentioning their encounter. After a few weeks of conversation, Jarrod felt Keith's resolve starting to fade. He knew his chance was coming, and this time he wouldn't let anything get in the way. Jarrod was willing to call it quits with the pastor he had been seeing for the last few months if Keith were open to a relationship. Nothing serious, he thought, just two old friends getting together and having some fun. Now all he had to do was convince Keith that if they were extra careful, no one would know.

*   *   *

When Jarrod finally emerged from the bathroom, Jackie pretended to be asleep. He settled into bed, and Jackie spun around to face him.

"Jarrod, I think we need to talk."

"Talk about what, Jackie? About how you put my mother in our business? Or about how you are not taking care of my house?"

"Jarrod, I don't want to argue with you. I just want us to be like we were before we were married. I want us to be happy again." She reached to touch his arm, but he moved just out of her reach.

"If you want to go back to being single, be my guest…"

"Jarrod, you know that's not what I meant…"

He cut her off. "Well, that's what you said. And if you want us to be happy, you can start by making me happy. First thing you can do is to stop playing the victim with all of this non-sense about being stressed out. You have nothing to stress about. You have the baby you wanted, the house, the car, and, need I say, a husband who pays for all of it. Oh, and while we're talking about things that will make me happy, you can keep my mother out of our business before you wind up alone and miserable just like her."

He pulled the blanket up to his neck and turned his back to her.

"I'm tired, and I've had a long day."

"Jarrod…" Jackie began.

"I said I'm tired. Let it go. There is nothing else to discuss."

Jackie got out of bed and went into the bathroom to cry in peace. She didn't understand why Jarrod treated her the way he did. It was like hated her. She looked at herself in the mirror and did not like the person staring back at her. She felt as though her dignity was being stripped from her. Jackie was never one to back down from a challenge except for when it came to Jarrod. She was getting tired of his whores calling her home and hanging up. Whenever she would bring it up, he would tell her she was imagining things. A few women would be so bold to ask for Jarrod when Jackie answered, and she would launch into a verbal attack, calling the women everything but a child of God. Lately Jarrod seemed to be more secretive than ever by sneaking away with his cell phone to the bathroom or his downstairs office to carry on late night conversations with someone. This hurt more than any of the others, because it seemed as though Jarrod was more preoccupied with this one. When Jackie received the latest bill, she saw one phone number that showed up repeatedly on Jarrod's cell phone bill. She noticed that Jarrod called these numbers late in the evening and early morning. Jackie decided to find out who the woman was on the other end of the phone. Jackie called the number repeatedly but never got an answer, only an answering machine with a mechanical voice so there was no chance of finding out her name until she actually spoke to her.

*   *   *

When Jackie arrived home from her meeting with Donna, she began preparing Jarrod's favorite meal: Filet Mignon, baked potatoes and asparagus. She decided to get to the bottom of what Donna told her once and for all. She planned on getting in touch with Keith first thing in the morning, because, as much as she wanted her marriage to work, she couldn't ignore the nagging feeling that her husband might be gay.

DONNA

"Hey Girl, what time can I come in today?" I asked Sabrina when she finally picked up the phone.

"Well, I'm finishing up my first customer now, so if you can get here in the next half hour, I can squeeze you in. What are you getting?"

"I want a touch up, and you can layer it too."

"All right girl, you know I'll hook you up, but you need to get here before my next appointment comes in."

"Thank you, and I'll see you in a few, bye." I hung up the phone and put on a sweat suit. My hair was in no condition to be seen by anyone, so I put on a one of Keith's baseball caps and headed out the door. I looked at my watch. It was 10:30, which meant I had four hours to get my hair done, because Keith asked that I be ready at 7:30.

I was turning thirty years old the next day, and Keith made plans for us to go out that evening. He'd been really secretive about what he planned, but, knowing him, it would be memorable.

Twenty minutes later, I pulled in front of Sabrina's salon

on the north side of Broad St. I walked into the shop and noticed Sabrina already had another client in her chair.

When she saw me, she shrugged her shoulders and mouthed, "Sorry."

I said hello to everyone and sat down in a huff directly across from Sabrina's station. I knew I really couldn't complain, considering I didn't have an appointment in the first place, but that didn't stop me from impatiently tapping my foot on the floor just to aggravate her. For the last five years, I have kept an unofficial standing Saturday appointment with Sabrina. I never committed to a time. I would simply call her to see what time was good for her. While I waited, I picked up a two-year-old issue of *Ebony* magazine. I skimmed a few pages, but I decided if Sabrina caught me reading, she would think I was comfortable with waiting. I put the magazine down and stared at her until she looked up.

When she caught me looking, she called out to another stylist, "Stephanie, can you take Donna back and prep her, please?" She looked at me. "Let me finish up with this color, and I'll be ready for you."

It took another forty minutes before Sabrina made it over to start applying my relaxer, and another hour and a half before she finally started styling my hair. While I was in her chair, Sabrina made small talk about my birthday plans.

"So, what does Keith have planned for you tonight?"

"He won't tell me, but I'm sure it will be nice. A couple of weeks ago, he gave me his platinum card to go shopping and, girl, I had a ball." I said.

She turned my chair to face the mirror so I could see how she would style my hair. "You want long layers, right?"

I nodded.

"Girl, I need me a man like Keith. Shit, he got any friends with ends?" She laughed.

"He has some from that Black Men's League, but they ain't nothing you would want."

"I ain't picky, I just want somebody with a J-O-B. I am so tired of these broke-ass men out here trying to live off of me. And the ones with money ain't trying to give it up without something in return. Those days are over. That shit was cool when we were younger, running with a bunch of different dudes and fucking for sport. But now I'm ready to stop playing around and find me my knight in shining armor to sweep me off my feet and take care of me like Keith does for you."

She laughed out loud and gestured for me to slap her five, but I ignored her outstretched hand and sucked my teeth at her last comment.

"First of all, Keith doesn't take care of me, I take care of myself. He just helps out from time to time like a real man should. You just need to stop looking in all the wrong places. There are good men out here, and just like I met Keith, you can meet somebody too. I mean, nobody's perfect."

Sabrina actually had the nerve to roll her eyes at me in the mirror.

"First of all, you, the only reason you met Keith is because he stumbled into your office looking for that lawyer you work for. And don't forget, you chased him, not the other way around. So don't act like it was a fairytale. As far as where I meet my men doesn't matter. Men like Keith aren't waiting to meet women like me. They want them fake bitches."

She stopped and looked at me. I decided to keep my mouth shut, because the last thing I need is for this jealous bitch to get scissor happy.

Instead, I thanked her, handed over her money, and left.

*   *   *

My doorbell rang at exactly 7:30, and I took my time answering the door. Nothing like a little anticipation to keep him wanting more. I double-checked myself in the mirror, and I was pleased with my reflection. Once again, Sabrina had worked her magic.

If only she wasn't so hateful and miserable, I thought.

The dress I bought from the mall hugged my body like a glove, and I adjusted it to accentuate the body part Keith loved the most, my ass. When I was satisfied with my look, I open the door for Keith.

"Happy Birthday, baby," he said as he handed me two-dozen white, pink, and red roses. "You look beautiful."

Keith was dressed to perfection. He wore a tailored navy blue suit that complemented his physique perfectly.

I spun around. "You like?" Keith smiled in appreciation. "I hope so, because you paid for it." I laughed.

"Let's get going," Keith said as he helped me with my coat.

When we exited the building, I saw a stretch Lincoln Navigator waiting in the middle of my small street.

"Keith, you are too much," I said before kissing him.

All of my nosy neighbors were outside gaping at the huge car. I took that opportunity to show off and walk like I was on the red carpet.

"Stuck up ho," I heard someone whisper.

I turned and smiled at the crowd while Keith held the door for me. When we settled in the car, Keith popped open a bottle of Perrier Jouët and poured two glasses.

"Here's to a special birthday for a special woman."

"Thank you, sweetie. I can't believe you did all of this."

"You only turn thirty once, so sit back and enjoy the rest of your evening."

We arrived at the Four Seasons Hotel in Center City thirty minutes later. Keith escorted me inside and over to the bar in the Swann Lounge. He ordered a drink for me then excused himself. I hoped his idea of a great evening wasn't sitting at a bar and getting a hotel room.

"This is a nice hotel and all, but, damn, we could do this anytime," I said while attempting to get the attention of the bartender.

Already feeling tipsy from helping myself to the vodka in the limo, I changed my mind about the drink and turned to watch as Keith walked toward the reservation desk. I was startled by a tap on my shoulder.

"Hello. Donna, right?" I shivered at the sound of the deep sexy voice behind me.

I turned around to see Keith's father standing next to an older couple and a homely looking girl who was about my age.

"Yes. Hello, Mr. Reed." I forced a smile. I was very aware that Mr. Reed thought his son was too good for me. "Keith stepped away for a minute. He should be right back."

"Well, I saw you sitting here alone and I thought I would come over and say hello. My friends and I are about to be seated." He was staring at my legs a little too hard.

I cleared my throat to get his attention away from my thighs.

"Well, it was nice seeing you again, Mr. Reed, and I will tell Keith I saw you."

"You do that. Enjoy the rest of your evening."

I said goodbye to the old couple and the funny-looking girl as they headed toward their table.

Mr. Reed turned to look at me one more time before turning his attention back to his guests. *Dirty old man,* I thought. *What kind of shit was that? He damned near undressed me with his eyes. Under different circumstances, Mr. Reed could get some. He is a spitting image of Keith, only older and grayer, but age ain't nothing but a number. But he's Keith's father and my soon-to-be father-in-law, so I wouldn't go there, and neither should he.*

Keith interrupted my thoughts with a kiss on my neck. "Sorry I kept you waiting, baby. I had to take care of something."

"That's okay. Guess who I saw a few minutes ago?"

"Who?"

"Your father. He was with a stuffy old couple and some

girl. They are at the table behind you over there." I motioned with my head.

Keith grunted. "Maybe we can go upstairs without having to see him. I don't feel like being bothered with him right now. I'll see him tomorrow at the luncheon over at First Day Baptist. Tonight is all about you." He snuck a look at his father's table. "Did he see you?" he whispered.

"I saw him, actually he came over and said hello. He wasn't all that bad considering how he feels about me. At least go over and say hi to him. It would be rude if you didn't. And what are you whispering for? It's not like he can hear you."

"Sorry. All right, you're right. We can go and say our hellos, but only for a minute. I have something special planned for us."

We got up and headed over to Mr. Reed's table.

"Hi, Dad." Keith reached over and shook his father's hand then turned to his guests at the table. "Dr. and Mrs. Harper, good seeing you again, and, Celeste, congratulations on finishing law school."

Celeste blushed and glanced at me.

"Hello, Keith. Would you and Donna like to join us for dinner?" Mr. Reed offered.

"No thanks, we've got to get going. I just wanted to stop by and say hello."

"Oh, Keith," Mrs. Harper said "We haven't seen you in so long. Your father introduced us to your friend, Donna. Join us. I'm sure we can get an extra place setting for her."

Keith grabbed my hand and pushed it forward so they could get a good look at my rock.

"Donna is my fiancé." Keith stared at his father, who was smiling, "And I'm sorry, but we can't. I've already made plans for us. We are celebrating her birthday."

"Oh. Well, now, isn't that sweet," Mrs. Harper cooed. "You know, Keith, now that Celeste has graduated, she'll be looking for a house soon, and we would appreciate you doing the honors of showing her a few of your properties."

I looked at Celeste, and she looked away, embarrassed.

"I'm sure I can help her find something to her liking. Now, if you'll excuse us, it was nice seeing you again. Celeste, give me a call."

Once again I waved goodbye and had to stop myself from sticking my tongue out at Mr. Reed and his friends.

When we were on the elevator, I said, "Correct me if I'm wrong, but I think they were trying to hook you up with their frumpy daughter."

"I wouldn't be surprised. They've been trying to set us up since we were in high school together. We went out a few times, but it didn't work out."

"Well, why not?" I asked with an attitude.

Keith laughed. "Well, my dear, because you would be more Celeste's type than I would."

"Get the hell out of here! How do you know?"

"Because she told me one night while we were out. She made me promise not to tell, so it's our little secret."

"What is the world coming to?" I asked myself.

We finally reached our floor, and Keith led me to our room and unlocked the door. He picked me up and carried me in.

"What are you doing, Keith?" I shrieked.

"I'm trying to get some practice for our big day

He put me down once we reached the living room. I looked around and was impressed. "Welcome to the Royal Suite, madam," Keith said with a bow.

"This is beautiful, Keith," I gushed.

"Come on, let me take you on the grand tour."

The room had a full kitchen, living room and dining room with a wet bar. There were two-dozen roses in the living room. I walked slowly to the bedroom, trying to take it all in. In the daylight, I was sure the view would be great, because even in the dark I could make out the lights of the art museum. The master bedroom had a huge, canopied king size bed with tons of pink, white, and red rose petals covering it. The marble master bathroom was almost as big as my tiny apartment. We walked over to the second bedroom and saw a smaller version of the master bedroom. The only difference in there was a massage table set up, with a masseuse ready to go. I looked at Keith.

"What's this for?"

"It's for you, of course. I want you to be totally relaxed this evening, so I want you to change out of your clothes and enjoy."

I reached up and nibbled on his bottom lip, "You are the best baby."

While I got probably the best massage of my life, Keith left me to go back into the living room. He said he needed to finish making some preparations. I dozed off while the masseuse worked her magic and didn't wake up until I heard Keith close the front door.

A few moments later, he peeked his head in and said, "We're ready for you."

"We?"

"Just come on, nosy." Keith tipped the masseuse and led her out.

I hopped off the table and pulled on my robe. Keith was standing at the head of the dining room table, which had been set to look like a page out of *Better Homes and Garden* magazine. A waiter was there, ready to serve, standing next to a tray of food. I sat down in the chair Keith pulled for me. After Keith was seated, he nodded to the waiter to begin serving our food. We ate food that I couldn't even pronounce. Keith had pre-ordered everything so, as each course was served, he described to me what everything was. When he'd told me my entrée was duck, I nearly threw up, but after he convinced me to taste it, I loved it. Once dessert was served, Keith got up and went to the bedroom. When he emerged, he was carrying three small boxes and an envelope. Anxious to receive my gifts, I finished my cheesecake in record time. Keith sat the boxes down in front of me.

"What is it?" I asked excitedly.

"Open them."

I tore the first box open and in it was a diamond pendant necklace.

"Oh, Keith, you remembered."

I recently hinted to Keith that I would like a necklace to

complement new ring. Inside the second box were a pair of diamond and sapphire earrings that matched the necklace. I didn't know what to expect when I opened the third box, but I was pleasantly surprised when I saw a gold MasterCard complete with my own name in gold letters. I jumped into Keith's lap and gave him a sloppy kiss.

"I take it you like your gifts," Keith laughed against my kisses.

"Yes! Oh my God, Keith, I love everything!" I kissed him some more. "Thank you, thank you, thank you!"

I put my earrings on after admiring them some more while Keith helped me with the necklace. I picked up the card and asked, "What's the credit limit?"

"$5,000.00. I put you as an additional cardholder, so don't worry about the bill."

I excused the waiter and led Keith to the bedroom. I pushed him back on the bed and did a slow striptease. His appreciation was evident by the bulge in his pants. When I was finished, the only thing left on my body were my earrings, necklace and four-inch stilettos. I took Keith's shoes and shirt off, but he had to help me with his pants because his erection was straining against the material. I climbed on top of him, kissed his thighs, and teased him with my tongue until he begged for more. When I took him in my mouth, I couldn't help thinking about his sexuality and the fact that he had been inside of a man's ass. As I had done many times before, I pushed the thought out of my head and pushed on. When I felt Keith about to cum, I got up and straddled his face, wanting him to taste my wetness. He licked and sucked until I came on his face, almost smothering him. Keith lifted me up and placed me on top of him and put on a condom. As he entered me, I kissed him full on the mouth.

"I love you so much," he said.

I rode him slow and steady, just like he liked, and just before he came I jumped up and, in one swift movement, took off the condom and took him in my mouth once again, just in time to swallow his ejaculation. Keith screamed in shock and excitement. He always hinted that he would like me to do that, but I had always refused.

I laid there in silence, listening to Keith snore softly, while I fought the urge to run to the bathroom to gargle. It wasn't long before I snuggled in next to him and drifted off to sleep.

The next morning I woke up to Keith singing "Happy Birthday" and serving me breakfast in bed. We had another round of lovemaking before we headed out to the waiting limo.

"You really outdid yourself, Keith. I really enjoyed myself, and I love my gifts," I said. "I especially liked getting served breakfast in bed. It feels good to be pampered."

He smiled. "You deserve it, and you know." He took my hand, "If you moved in with me, there could be more where that came from."

"Keith, we talked about that. I really don't want to move in together until after the wedding."

"I know, baby, but that's my point. We know we're getting married, so what's the big deal? Besides, I don't like the idea of my soon-to-be wife living in the hood when my house is big enough for a family of six. Come on, Donna, you know it's not safe where you are, and I wouldn't be able to stand it if something happened to you."

He looked at me expectantly, but I remained silent.

"All right, how about this," he continued. "If you don't want to move in with me yet, at least move into one of my buildings. There is a vacant apartment in the duplex on Union Avenue, over in Yeadon. "

I sighed. "Let me think about it, okay?"

He nodded and kissed my hand. "Don't be so stubborn. Let me do this for you."

When we pulled in front of my apartment building, Keith walked me to my door and kissed me goodbye.

"I wish I didn't have to leave you, but I have to get ready to head over to the church for the luncheon. I'll call you when I'm done. Love you."

"Love you, too." I kissed him goodbye and went inside.

The first thing I noticed was the blinking red light on my answering machine. I listened to my mother ask for money, and, as an afterthought, she eventually said, "Happy birthday." Next was a message from Leah, Sabrina's sister, inviting me out to a new club that was opening up downtown the following weekend. The last message was a surprise. It took me a minute to place the voice, but it was Jackie. She left her cell phone number asking me to give her a call back. I decided to call her last, because I wasn't sure what was going on so soon. I called my mother first to find out why she needed money again.

"Hi, Mom. I got your message."

"Hey girl, where you been? I been calling you since last night."

"I was out with Keith for my birthday. I just came home."

"I know it's your birthday. Shit, I'm the one who had you. What'd you get? I'll get you something when I get my check."

Yeah right, I thought. "Some jewelry and a credit card. Oh, and Keith asked me to move in with him again."

"And? What did you say? Don't tell me you said no again."

I could almost see my mother standing with her hand on her hip and her neck rolling.

"I told him I would think about it."

"What he hell is wrong with you? Why not?"

"Because I don't want to live together until after the wedding. What do they say? Why buy the cow when you can get the milk for free?"

"Girl, please, Keith can buy and sell your ass. You keep on thinking that man is going to keep waiting around for your behind to come to your senses. What you need to do is pack your shit up, move in that house of his, and have his baby as soon as you can."

I shook my head. That was her answer for everything. If anyone asked her how to keep a man around, she would say, have his baby. I couldn't believe all of this relationship advice from a woman who had three children by three different men, none of whom stayed around. My mother was what I would call an O.G., an Original Gold-Digger. Unlike most mothers, who want their daughters to succeed by going to college, having a career, and moving up the corporate ladder, Irene Tate was just the opposite. Her idea of success was for me to snag a rich man, have his babies, and shower *her* with gifts. She instilled that gold digging mentality in me at a young age, but, lucky for me, I realized I couldn't put a price tag on my dignity. Shit, if I was going to sell my body, I would make sure the average man couldn't afford it.

"Mom, you said you needed money. What's wrong now?" I wanted to change the subject before an argument started.

"They cut my cable off on Friday, and Kevin ran my damn phone bill up accepting those collect calls from your trifling-ass jailbird brother."

"Well, why don't you make Kevin pay the bill then? Why do I always have to bail you out?"

"Kevin doesn't have any money, and he ain't found a job yet."

"What do you mean, he doesn't have any money? Every time I see him, he has on brand new sneakers and clothes. And the reason he doesn't have a job yet is because he doesn't want one. And he's too busy selling them drugs."

"First of all, he's not selling drugs anymore, and, if he is, I don't want that dirty money."

"Why not? He lives there, doesn't he? And you don't seem to have a problem with that dirty money when he buys your cigarettes with it or when you need Bingo money."

So much for avoiding an argument.

"Look, are you going to give it to me or not? I ain't got time for this. I need my cable, and I ain't even got call waiting on my phone no more, so you tying up my line."

"Nope. Sorry, Mom, but I don't have it right now. Besides, I'm not going to keep helping you when you won't ask Kevin. He's a grown man, and you are ruining him because you won't make him act like it."

"What you mean you ain't got it right now? What about that credit card you said Keith gave you?"

"Mom, that is for me. I haven't even gotten a chance to use it for myself yet."

"You know what? I am so sick of this high and mighty shit you on now. You can't even help your own mother out in an emergency? You better hope you never need me for nothing, 'cause I'm a remember this shit."

"It ain't like you ever helped me anyway," I said under my breath.

"What you just say?"

"Mom, getting your cable cut off and not having call waiting is not what I consider an emergency. You'll survive, and since you don't want to ask Kevin, just get it cut on when you get your check."

"I got other stuff I gotta do when I get my check, but you know what? Just forget it." She slammed the phone down in my ear.

"Whatever, you'll need me before I need you," I said to the phone.

Next, I called Leah. I hoped she could take my mind off of the bullshit with my mother. She answered on the first ring.

"Hey, birthday girl!"

"Hey, girl, what's up?"

"Are you coming out with us next weekend? Power 99 is

going to be at the opening of Club Apollo and you know it's gonna be bananas."

I thought back to the argument Sabrina and I had the day before and how stank she acted.

"I don't know, Leah, it sounds like fun but…"

"Girl, I know you ain't about to say no. Yeah, yeah, yeah I heard all about you and my sister arguing, but so what? I'm inviting you, and plus y'all always going through something, so what else is new?"

"Well, I haven't been out in a while, and I do need to shake my ass a little," I laughed.

"That's what's up. All right, you can meet us at the club at eleven o'clock. It's on 3rd and Market, okay?"

"Okay, see you then." I hung up and hoped I wouldn't regret my decision to hang out with them. Sabrina and I have had arguments before, but nothing as personal as what happened yesterday.

Finally, I called Jackie, and when she picked up the phone she sounded rushed.

"Hey Jackie, it's Donna. I just got your message."

"Hey, I really can't talk now, Jarrod just walked in. I just want Keith's cell number because I want to ask him a few questions."

"Sure. You want it now?"

"Um, can you call me back and leave it on my voicemail? I don't want to write it down."

"Okay, no problem. But he's not going to be home today.

He's going over to First Day Baptist for some men's day luncheon they're having."

"Yeah I know. Jarrod's going too."

"Oh yeah? Well, I'll let you go. Hang up, and I'll call back and leave the number.

"Okay, thanks."

Just thinking about Keith and Jarrod being in the same place at the same time had me beyond pissed, because he neglected to mention Jarrod's being at the luncheon.

After I called and left Keith's cell number on Jackie's voicemail, I called Keith and prayed that he had not turned off his cell phone.

When he answered, I asked, "Did you forget to tell me that Jarrod would be at the *men's* luncheon at the church, or did you conveniently forget?"

"Hello to you too, Donna. And no, I didn't know he would be there. I'm not surprised though, most of the brothers from the league will be there. Why, what's wrong?"

"What do you think is wrong, Keith? How would you like it if I was going to be spending the day with the man *or* woman I cheated with?"

"Baby, you have nothing to worry about. I haven't talked to Jarrod since I changed my numbers, and I won't be spending the day with him. There will be at least a hundred men there."

"For some reason knowing that doesn't make me feel too secure either, Keith."

He sighed loudly into the phone. "There is no need for

that, Donna. Please trust me on this, you have nothing to worry about."

"Whatever, Keith. Don't fuck up, and I ain't playing."

"I promise, baby. I love you, and I'll call you when I get in."

"Bye."

I started to call him back to cuss him out for rushing me off the phone, but changed my mind.

I hated feeling this way, always wondering if my man was going to fall into bed with the next fine brother that crossed his path. I don't think I knew what the hell I was getting myself into thinking I could stay with a man who probably has the same taste in as men as me.

KEITH

After I hung up with Donna, I turned off the ringer on my cell phone. I could understand her apprehension about Jarrod, but I also needed her to trust me. I walked into the large church and was greeted by my father, who was speaking with Pastor Douglas' wife, Ms. Elaine.

"Here's Keith now," my father said.

"Hello, Keith," Ms. Elaine said. "Well, I guess I will leave you two boys alone, and, Harold," she added as she turned back to my father, "I will speak with you later."

I briefly waved to Ms. Elaine and turned away. To look at her one would never know that she gave new meaning to the term "giving head." Ever since I caught her and my father squeezed together in the port-a-potty at last year's church picnic, I could barely look at her without thinking of seeing her swallow my father's member whole. She could have made millions as the next Deep Throat.

"Glad you could make it, Son," he said as he stared at Mrs. Douglas's ass.

I silently wished Pastor Douglas would round the corner

and catch my father ogling his wife's ass. Thinking of the pastor beating on my father made me smile.

"Wouldn't miss it for the world."

He turned his attention back to me. "You know, I think Celeste is really looking forward to looking at those properties with you. Dr. Harper told me she's not dating anyone." He winked at me.

"You know, you could always date her. Or did she turn you down already?"

"I don't appreciate you speaking to me like that, Keith. Have some respect. I'm your father and I only want what's best for you."

"Thanks, but no thanks, Dad. I'm very happy with Donna, and I'm sure Celeste doesn't need you and her parents running interference on whom she dates. We are friends, and I intend on keeping it that way," I said as I turned to walk away.

I walked into the basement and greeted Pastor Douglas and a few of the deacons before settling in at a nearby table.

The ceremony lasted for about two hours, and after the final collection was taken, the food was finally served. I dug into my overflowing plate of ribs, catfish, collard greens, macaroni and cheese, stuffing, potato salad, yams, and cornbread. A few of the brothers from the league were at my table, and we indulged in idle chit-chat until someone brought up the upcoming AIDS awareness fundraiser.

"So, how many tickets have you sold?" Larry, the league's treasurer, asked me.

"Man, I'm not even gonna lie. There's been so much going on lately it totally slipped my mind."

"You better get on it. It'll be here before you know it. And you know this year you are responsible for either purchasing or selling however many tickets you committed to."

"Shit — oh, excuse me," I said as I looked at the ceiling, "I forgot. I'll see if I can get a few of the brothers over at the barbershop to buy some."

The conversation continued for several more minutes until I grew weary. I knew that if I sat still any longer I would fall asleep, so I excused myself and went to mingle for a bit. On my way to the restroom, I spotted Pastor Douglas coming out of his office with Jarrod so I spun around and headed toward the exit. I said a few goodbyes on my way out, but just as I made it to the door, I heard Jarrod yelling for me to stop.

"Yo, Keith, wait up." I kept walking. "Keith! What's up man, you in a rush?" he asked as he caught up with me.

"Yeah, I gotta get home. Donna and I had a late night and I'm beat."

"What's going on? I tried calling you, but your numbers are disconnected, so I left you a couple messages at the office. So what's up, didn't you get the messages?"

"Nothing's up. Look, Jarrod, I have to get going," I said while trying to walk around him.

He blocked my path. "So you still trying to get together or what?"

"Nah, man, I don't think that's going to happen. I shouldn't have even let my mind go that way."

"What way? What's that supposed to mean?" He was getting angry.

"It means that I love Donna, and I'm not messing that up again. So I'm sorry if I made it seem like it was something it wasn't, but I made a promise to Donna that I intend to keep."

"Are you serious? How is she going to know?"

I started to tell him about Jackie calling my home, but decided against it. I couldn't be sure how he would react, and I didn't want him to take it out on Jackie.

"That's not the point. She is going to be my wife and the only person I want to be with."

"You know what your problem is? She's got you pussy-whipped."

He stood in front of me with an aggressive stance and his nostrils were flaring.

I shook my head and laughed. "Maybe so, but that's not the only reason I'm not dealing with you, Jarrod. I'm sure Pastor Douglas is still good for some fun, so why don't you stick with a sure thing? Do me a favor, don't call me anymore. Oh, and tell Jackie I said hello."

I pushed past him and made my way to my truck before he could say anymore. When I got in the car, I checked my cell and saw that I missed two calls, one from Donna and another from a number I did not recognize. I turned the ringer back on and returned Donna's call first.

"Hey, baby, I see I missed your call."

"Yeah, I'm thinking about coming over tonight and I called to see if you want me to cook?"

Although her voice still held a hint of attitude, I was glad to hear she wasn't as pissed as she was earlier.

"Damn, I wish you had said that earlier before I ate all of that food. Can we do it tomorrow?"

"I guess, depending on how I feel when I get off work. So how was the luncheon?"

"It was cool. By the time Pastor Douglas finished thanking us for all of the work we've done in the community and then digging in our pockets, I was hungry as hell." I laughed, "I think they did it that way on purpose. Starve us so we would give damn near anything to eat some food."

"Yeah, Pastor Douglas has a way of making you dig deeper and deeper in your pockets. That church is about as bad as going to Atlantic City."

"You got that right. So, you still coming over?"

"Do you want me to come over?"

"Yeah, if you want to come over."

She let out a loud groan. "I asked if you *want* me to come over."

"Yes, Donna, I want you to come over. I always want you to come over. Shit, I want you to move in."

"All right. I'll be there around eight."

"Okay, baby. See you then."

"Keith!" I heard Donna calling me just as I was about to hang up the phone.

"Yes?"

"I forgot to tell you, Jackie called me earlier and asked me for your cell number."

"Did she say why?"

"She just said she wants to ask you a few questions."

That must have been the other missed call, I thought. It was my turn to groan. "You gave it to her?"

"Yes, I did. Why wouldn't I?"

"Because I don't want to get involved in their marriage, that's why."

"Well, you involved yourself the day you let him suck your..."

"All right, Donna, I got you. I'll see you when you get there." I saw where the conversation was headed, and I didn't want to go there with her.

"Are you going to call her back?"

"Yeah, I will."

"When?"

"When I get a chance."

"Don't get an attitude with me. You drew first blood by even being with him, now you have to deal with it."

"I don't have an attitude, Donna, I'm just trying to move on with my life, that's all. I'll see you later. Love you."

"Love you too, bye."

I looked at Jackie's number again and deleted it. The last thing I wanted to do was to share that part of myself with someone else. Maybe she would give up trying if I didn't respond. I decided at that moment to screen my calls and forget about both Jackie and Jarrod. I turned the music up and headed home.

DONNA

Keith convinced me to stay the entire week at his house. When I left his house for work on Monday morning, he asked me to do a trial run of cohabitation, as he put it, to see if he could change my mind about moving in. After work, I went to my apartment to get enough clothing and toiletries to last the week.

By Friday, Keith had just about sold me on the idea of moving in. He'd gone out of his way to make sure he tended to my every need. He would not let me lift a finger. Every night, Keith made sure to get home earlier than usual to either cook dinner or make reservations. Our evenings were spent cuddling up to watch a good movie and retiring to the bedroom to enjoy each other's company. Although I knew this would not happen every day of our marriage, I couldn't help but get even more excited about what life would be like after the wedding. After our trial period was over, I promised Keith I would seriously consider coming to live with him.

On Saturday morning, I swallowed my pride and called Sabrina to see what time she wanted me to come in. It took a lot of deliberation on my part to give in and call her, but I figured since we were all going to go out, things between us were cool. When I called the shop, Jasmine, the receptionist, answered on the first ring.

"Thank you for calling In The Cut. How can I help you?"

"Hey, Jazzy, it's Donna. Is Sabrina there?"

"Um, hey, Donna. Hold on." She put the phone down and I heard her talking to Sabrina in the background.

"Donna?" Jazzy picked the phone back up.

"Yes?"

"She said she's booked today, so you'll have to make an appointment for next week."

"What! She's booked? Where she at?"

"She's putting color in a client's hair, and she said she can't come to the phone." I could tell she was getting uncomfortable with the whole conversation, so I let her off the hook.

"It's cool, I'll call her cell. Thanks, Jazzy."

"Bye."

"Bye."

I couldn't believe this evil bitch was acting like that. I called her cell, and she must have hit "ignore" when saw it was me because it went straight to voicemail. I called over and over again, but she would not answer.

Finally, I said, "Fuck it, I got a trick for her ass."

I decided to call the salon directly across the street from hers. Sabrina absolutely hated the owner, Sheena, because she had everything Sabrina did not, including a few of Sabrina's former clients. For starters, Sheena's salon was full-service, offering manicures, pedicures, spa treatments, and a barber on premises. Sheena also owned the building that housed her salon, while Sabrina was still sleeping with the very married landlord of her building for a discount on rent.

Lucky for me, Sheena had a cancellation, so I was able to get an appointment for two o'clock.

I made sure to park in front of Sabrina's shop so she could get a good look at me. When I got out of the car, I saw Sabrina looking my way and rolling her eyes at me, so I made a big production of walking toward the parking meter so she would think I was coming in. The look on her face was priceless when she saw me double back to go across the street to Sheena's salon. I would have killed to hear what she was saying about me.

True to her reputation, Sheena hooked my hair up. I ran my fingers through my hair as I walked to my car and laughed when I saw Sabrina staring me down. I debated on whether or not I should call Leah and tell her I wouldn't be coming tonight. I was feeling good despite the mess that happened with Sabrina, and the last thing I wanted was to go out and have her ruin it. Between seeing Sabrina pissed off and me feeling sexy as hell with my new look, my mood had lifted considerably by the time I got home, so I decided to go with them anyway. I figured the club would be big enough for me to go and do my own thing without having to deal with Sabrina's hateful ass. Besides, it had been too long since the last time I had been out without Keith hanging around.

The clock in my bedroom read 6:12, which left me just enough time to take a quick nap, get changed, and be out of the house by 10:15. Even though Leah said we'd meet at 11:00, I knew that parking downtown on a Saturday night would be a bitch, so I knew I needed to leave early.

I awoke from my nap with an hour left to get ready. I scarfed down a turkey and cheese sandwich and spent the majority of my time soaking in the tub. My red mini dress and red strappy stilettos were the perfect outfit for a night at the club. Even though it was early April and the nights were not yet warm, I refused to be covered head to toe. All I had left to do was choose some jewelry and, thanks to Keith, I had plenty to choose from. I decided on a pair of 1½ carat diamond stud earrings and the necklace Keith gave me for my birthday. I just knew I was the shit until I looked in the mirror and noticed a nasty panty line staring back at me. I would normally wear a thong to avoid situations such as these, but tonight it wasn't working. At the last minute, I decided to take the thong off and, viola, perfection. I blew a kiss to my reflection and was on my way. It was 10:35, so I knew I had to get moving before got too crowded, and by then, it would be damn near impossible to find Leah. I put on my coat and grabbed my keys just as the phone rang.

Ring!

I looked at the caller ID and saw it was Keith.

Ring!

I thought about letting the machine pick it up, but I knew that would only make him blow my cell up all night.

"Hello?" I made sure to say it in a way that would let him know I was in a hurry.

"What's up, you busy or something?"

"I'm on my way out the door."

"This late? Where are you going?"

"Out with Sabrina, Leah, and Tanya. I told you that yesterday. We're going to that new club downtown."

"Maybe you did. But anyway, I just wanted to check in with you because I haven't heard from you all day. I missed you. I'm so used to you being here, and now the house feels empty."

I knew he was trying to make me feel guilty for not calling him so I would stay in with him. But I wasn't having it. My heart was set on going out, and I had no plans on doing anything other than that.

"I'm sorry, but I was busy. I had to find somebody to do my hair, and by the time I got home, I had just enough time to take a nap and get ready."

"Doesn't your girl Sabrina do your hair?"

"Yeah, she used to." I was beginning to get impatient. "It's a long story, though. I'll tell you about it later. Let me get out of here, I'll call you if it's not too late when I get in."

"All right, baby. Enjoy yourself, and be careful. I love you."

"You too, bye."

I made it to the club at 11:30 and, just like I thought, parking was hell and the club was packed.

I figured Leah must have given up on me and gone inside, so I went right in. As soon as I walked in, I heard the DJ mixing up some of my favorite old school jams, so I immediately fell into step with the dancing crowd. Before I knew it, I danced through three songs straight, so after promising my new dance partner that I would return, I went to find Sabrina and her sisters. I looked around the club for any large groups of men, because nine times out of ten Sabrina could be found in a circle of men. Leah and Tanya were standing near the bar talking to three men who looked old enough to be their daddy, but Sabrina was nowhere around. Tanya noticed me first and waved me over.

"Hey girl, we didn't think you were coming," she said as she reached for a hug. She gave the man she was talking to her phone number and promised to call.

"I know, but Keith called me when I was halfway out the door." I turned to nudge Leah. "Hey Leah, how you doin'?"

Leah ended her conversation with the old man and turned to me, "Is this shit off the hook or what?"

"Yeah, the DJ is doing his thing."

"I'll be right back. I need a drink. Y'all want anything?" I asked.

Leah handed me her glass. "Yeah, get me a Henny and Coke."

I turned to Tanya "Nah, I'm good. I'm feeling a little tipsy as it is."

Leah rolled her eyes. "Her corny ass could never hold her liquor anyway."

I shrugged my shoulders, said, "Suit yourself," and walked to the bar.

"Can I get a Grey Goose and cranberry and a Hennessey and Coke?" I asked when I got the barmaid's attention.

I took the drinks and said a silent prayer that no one would bump into me as I walked back. I made it back safely with our drinks, but had to wait until Leah finished grinding on some guy who couldn't have been any more than twenty-two.

When the song ended, she took her drink and said, "I used to fuck with his older brother Derrick, but, shit, I think I'm feeling him now. He's all grown up now. Looks just like his brother did."

"You know you ain't right," I laughed.

"Why not? Derrick died three years ago, so what's the harm? I'm just trying to have a little fun."

"If you say so." I shook my head at her because I knew trying to school her on right from wrong was fruitless.

"Where's Tanya?"

"Right here," Tanya said walking up behind me. "I had to pee, and that damned line to the women's bathroom was long as hell, so I snuck into the men's bathroom."

"Look, Tanya, Sabrina's still over there talking to that dude she met earlier. She must like this one, 'cause she been in his face since we got here," Leah said as she pointed.

"He is fine. though. I wish I would have seen him first."

I looked over to where Leah was pointing and nearly choked on my drink when I saw who she was talking to. Standing next to her with his hand on her ass was Jarrod.

"What's going on with you and Sabrina anyway, Donna?" Tanya asked.

I couldn't take my eyes off of Sabrina and Jarrod laughing and talking.

"Nothing, why do you ask?"

"Because I was at the shop earlier when you called and then I saw you go over to Sheena's salon."

I shrugged my shoulders, "Well, when I called for my appointment, she said she couldn't take me, and I needed my hair done, so I went to Sheena."

"Y'all two are always going through something," Leah said, rolling her eyes, "ever since y'all were little."

"So, do you know the guy she's over there talking to?" I asked them.

"Nope, she met him as soon as we walked in and has been with him ever since," Tanya said.

"I saw her in the bathroom a little while ago, and she told me he's a lawyer. So I think this one's a keeper." Leah laughed. "You never know, she may have finally found her knight in shining armor."

As much as Sabrina knew how to get under my skin, I still didn't want her to be mixed up with a sick bastard like Jarrod. She looked so happy just to be in his presence. I hated to be the one to burst her bubble. But I had to tell her he was no good. The only problem was how to tell her about Jarrod without exposing Keith. I decided to tell her that he's married with a baby on the way, which wasn't a lie. Although I doubted that piece of information would matter, because Sabrina was known for sleeping with plenty of married men. It seemed like, after Lance, she went out of her way to sleep around. But, yet and still, she was my girl, and I wouldn't be any kind of friend if I didn't tell her

"Why are you so quiet?" Leah asked me.

"Because I know him. He's an old friend of Keith's."

"Well, that's good, I'm sure Keith wouldn't hang with anybody who doesn't have it going on. Maybe you two can double date," Tanya said.

"No it's not good, and we will definitely never double date."

"Damn, it's like that? Why are you hatin' on her and her dude like that?" Leah asked with an attitude.

"Yeah, it's like that, because I'm sure his pregnant wife would be very upset." I looked at both of them to see their reactions.

"Are you serious?" Tanya asked.

"Very," I said.

"Well, we gotta tell her," Tanya said. "That's messed up."

"What difference does it make?" Leah asked, "How do you know if they are even still together? He don't look married to me, and if he is, so what? He must not be happy if he's out at a club."

"Shut up, Leah. I'm going to get her." Tanya pushed past us, marched right over to Sabrina and grabbed her arm. Sabrina looked ready to kill Tanya and snatched her arm back. She must have told Jarrod to wait because I saw him nod his head and smile. I could hear Sabrina cussing Tanya out the entire way over to where we were standing. I looked back over to where Jarrod was standing and we locked eyes. He must have put two and two together because the expression on his face went from smug to angry almost instantly.

Tanya pushed Sabrina in my face and said, "Donna has something to tell you."

Sabrina sucked her teeth, "She ain't got shit to say to me."

"Sabrina, cut it out and listen to what she has to say. Go ahead, Donna."

I sighed. "That guy you are talking to is an old friend of Keith's and…"

"So?" She rolled her eyes and crossed her arms.

"And he's married with a baby on the way," Tanya finished.

"That's what the hell you pulled me over here for?"

"Yeah…" Tanya said.

"I thought you should know." I said

"Mind your damn business!" She yelled, "He already told me that. What, you think I'm stupid? He's wearing a ring."

"And that's okay with you?" Tanya asked shaking her head.

"Why the hell not? I'm enjoying myself and so is he. As a matter of fact, he told me he's getting divorced too." She turned to me. "Did you know that, big mouth?"

Sabrina was raising her voice so loud that even the music couldn't hide it, and people were beginning to stare.

"See, I told y'all to leave it alone," Leah said.

"Look, whatever. Do what you want," I said, shrugging my shoulders.

Sabrina had one hand in my face and the other on her hip. "I don't need your permission."

"What the hell is your problem, Sabrina? I'm trying to

help you, and all you are doing is giving me your ass to kiss. But, you know what? Fuck it. Fuck him, and fuck you too. I am so sick of you and your pissy-ass attitude. Let him dog you out, just like the rest of them."

The people near us must have sensed trouble, because I saw the crowd of spectators growing.

"No." She wagged her finger in my face. "Fuck you Donna, with your stuck-up ass. Stop trying to act like you are some goody-fuckin' two-shoes. Don't act like you ain't never messed with a married man. Shit, you was screwin' your boss the last time you and Keith broke up. And correct me if I'm wrong, but isn't he married?"

Tanya and Leah were struck silent. They were used to Sabrina and me having a bunch of disagreements, but it never got to this point. Tanya stepped in between us before it got out of hand.

"What is going on with you two? People are staring at you!" she hissed.

"So, let 'em stare," Sabrina said. True to form, she always loved being the center of attention, good or bad.

"I know you are not going to let a man cause all of this trouble. Is he really worth it, Sabrina?" Tanya asked.

"Look, I don't need to explain myself to none of y'all, especially this ho right here," she said as she flicked her wrist in my face. "Do me a favor, the next time we go out, leave the trash at home. I gotta get back to my new man."

The crowd parted as she walked back over to Jarrod. Disappointed because there was no fight to see, the crowd thinned.

Jarrod met my stare just as Sabrina slid into his arms. He wore that same self-satisfied smirk as the day I caught him with Keith. I had the overwhelming urge to slap it off, but instead I decided to call it a night.

"All right y'all, I'm out. I've had enough excitement for one night. "

Tanya and I hugged, but when I turned to Leah, she didn't budge.

"What wrong with you?" I asked.

"Now I see what Sabrina was talking about."

"What are you talking about?"

"You *are* fake. His wife is not your friend, Sabrina is. If she's happy, then you should be happy for her. Fuck him and his wife."

"You know what, Leah? I really don't have time for this petty mess. If your sister thinks Jarrod is going to make her happy, then she is sadly mistaken. But that is not my problem anymore. I'm done."

On the way home, I thought about all of the things Sabrina and I have been through. After the way she acted at the club, not to mention the salon, I knew our friendship would never be the same.

The scene on my street was like something out of a movie, with ambulances, police cruisers, news vans and a large crowd of people. Unable to park on my street, I parked around the corner and walked. You can always tell when it's getting warm, I thought, because people start acting up. The presence of cops and ambulances didn't worry me, because that was the norm in my neighborhood. I stopped to ask Joyce, a neighbor from a few houses down, what was going on. My skin went cold when she told me there had been a home invasion of the first-floor apartment in my building. I looked around for the guy, Dante, who lived in the apartment, but I didn't see him anywhere. Joyce told me she heard about ten gunshots earlier, and then, next thing she knew, the police were all over the place.

"Where's Dante. Is he all right?" I asked.

"I don't think so. I saw a homicide detective go in there a while ago."

"Did anybody see anything?"

Joyce looked at me as though I had lost my mind, "What do you think? You know how it is. If they did, ain't nobody sayin' nothing. It's a shame, though. It ain't even hot yet."

"This is the second time this happened. Last year, Dante told me somebody broke in while he was asleep and stole his television and his house keys. We had to change all of the locks after that."

Joyce shook her head, "Come on Donna, be for real. You know what that boy is into. This don't have nothing to do with a TV. All of them people he had in and out of that apartment, you know he was hustling." I nodded my head in agreement.

"I'm going to go over there and see if they'll let me into my apartment. I'll talk to you later."

I made it up the first two steps before I was stopped by a police officer.

"Stand back, ma'am," the officer said.

"I live upstairs." I peeked over his head and saw another detective standing over top of a man's naked bloody body.

"I'm sorry, but this is a crime scene, and we cannot let anyone pass."

We were pushed to the side as two EMT workers wheeled an empty stretcher out of the apartment. Moments later, two body bags were brought out, and I had to turn my head. The thought that in one of those bags was my neighbor was enough to make me sick to my stomach. After exchanging a few more words with the officer, who still refused to let me in my apartment to get a few of my belongings, I drove over to Keith's house. While driving, I made up my mind to take Keith up on his offer and move in with him. Crime had become a way of life in my neighborhood, but knowing that I could have just as easily been the victim in the robbery left me shaken up.

Keith woke up as I climbed into bed with him. He smiled and wrapped his arms around me. "This is a nice surprise. I wasn't expecting to see you tonight."

No longer able to hold back the tears, I sobbed into his chest.

"Donna? What's wrong? What happened?"

I tearfully told him about everything starting with my fight with Sabrina, seeing her at the club with Jarrod, and then the murder in my building.

"Aw, baby, are you okay?" He asked.

I shook my head, "Does the offer still stand for me to move in?"

He took my face into his hands. "Of course it does. We'll go back to your apartment tomorrow and get your things."

"Tonight was horrible. Sabrina was being a real bitch, and to top it off, I come home to find that two people were killed in my building. I can't help thinking what could have happened if I had been home. What if they had tried to come into my apartment?" I asked tearfully.

"Baby, I think whoever it was came especially for Dante and whatever he was selling. I hate to say it, but I'm not surprised."

"Yeah, but I could have been home, or worse, walked in as it was happening."

"Thank God you weren't home, and thank you for finally coming to your senses about that neighborhood."

"Excuse me?" I found his statement to be offensive.

"Not like that Donna. I meant…forget it. Let's get some sleep and we can talk about it in the morning. Good night, baby. I love you," He kissed my lips and squeezed me a little tighter.

"You too. G'nite."

The next morning, Keith and I watched the morning news while eating breakfast. On the screen was the same scene I had witnessed just a few hours before. According to the detective being interviewed, two men were found shot to death inside of the apartment. The police believed there were at least two men involved in the home invasion, and one of the men found dead was one of the assailants. Along with several high-caliber guns and $16,000 in cash, police discovered three pounds of marijuana and crack cocaine worth about $10,000 on the street. I looked at

Keith and shivered. I knew that Dante' dabbled in selling marijuana. Sabrina and I would cop some from him on occasion, but I had no idea he was into the heavier drugs. It made me feel a little better knowing that the robbery and Dante's murder wasn't random, but I knew I would never feel comfortable living there after what happened.

On the drive over to my apartment, I asked Keith if he'd talked to Jackie.

"No, I haven't had a chance to call her yet."

"You haven't had a chance, or didn't want to?"

"Donna, please don't start. I'm trying to enjoy my day with you. I'll talk to her when I get a chance."

I opened my mouth to respond, but was cut off by the ringing of my cell phone. I looked at the display, "Speak of the devil," I said as I looked at Keith.

"Hey, Jackie," I said into the phone.

Keith looked pale but kept his eyes glued to the road.

"Hi, Donna. How've you been?"

"Other than my neighbor being killed in my building last night, I'm fine."

"Oh my God! That is horrible. Are you ok?"

"Mm-hmm, yeah, but enough about me. I should be asking you that question."

"Hold on a sec," Jackie said. She put the down and exchanged a few words with someone in the background. When she picked the phone up, I heard a baby crying.

"Sorry about that," she said. "I guess you can tell what I'm calling for."

"Oh my goodness, you had the baby? Congratulations! Okay, so tell me, what did you have, what's the name, and, oh God, did it hurt?" I was talking a mile a minute, barely giving her a chance to answer.

Jackie was laughing, "Thank you, and I had a girl. Her name is Naomi, and she is the cutest baby in the world. And, girl, yes, it hurt like hell."

"What hospital are you in?"

"I'm at Cooper, but I've been in here since Friday, so I'll be leaving tomorrow morning."

"Aww, I wish I could've seen you and the baby before you went home."

"It's okay. The only reason I stayed this long is because of my blood pressure. I'm sure you've heard how it is. These hospitals usually kick you out the day after the baby is born. But anyway, Jarrod is picking me up tomorrow, so you can come by the house...never mind."

There was an uncomfortable silence on the phone for a few seconds.

"Well, maybe we can do lunch one day soon. I do want to see the baby."

"That sounds like a plan. All right, let me go. I need to see if I can get in touch with Jarrod."

I thought about telling her about Jarrod and Sabrina, but she seemed so happy, and I didn't want to be the one to ruin that. "Okay, call me if you need anything."

"I will. Oh, Donna?"

"Uh-huh?"

"Do you know if Keith got any of my messages? He hasn't returned my calls."

I looked at Keith, who tensed as though he knew he was now the topic of our conversation.

"I'm going to see him this evening, and I will make sure he calls you back, ok?"

"Ok, thanks. Tell him, I'm not mad at him, I just need to know the truth."

After I closed my cell phone, I looked at Keith, who seemed to know what was coming next.

"I'll call her this week, Donna," he said.

I turned my head away from him without saying anything and we rode in silence the rest of the way to my apartment.

KEITH

"What are you doing home so soon?" Donna asked while standing at the top of the stairs.

I kissed her on he cheek and said, "What do you mean? Am I supposed to call first?"

I had just returned home from the gym and was anxious to get into the shower.

She blocked my path with outstretched arms, "No, but I wanted to surprise you, and now you ruined it."

"Surprise me with what?"

"I was doing some redecorating in the bedroom."

It had been a month since Donna moved in, and things were going well. She came in and made herself at home by re-decorating and settling in as the woman of the house.

"So are you going to let me pass or what?" I looked at her still-outstretched arms.

"Okay, but before you go in, close your eyes."

I sighed. "Is this really necessary?"

"Close them," she said. I closed my eyes and allowed her to lead me into the bedroom.

She stopped me and said, "Okay, you can open them."

I looked around the bedroom and saw that she had completely redecorated. The once almost bare dresser was now covered with candles, African American figurines, and two flower vases. There was even a new lavender and mint-green flower print bedspread with curtains to match. I was a little overwhelmed with the changes, because there was no sign of my original décor.

"So? What do you think? I have some ideas about the living room and kitchen too."

Donna stood in front of me with an expectant smile, and I didn't want to ruin her mood, so I lied. "It's…it's nice."

"You sure? Tell me if you don't like it. I promise I won't be mad."

Yeah right, I thought.

"I like it if you like it. I am leaving the decorating up to you. Do your thing, baby. Just let me get out of these clothes and take a shower. Then you can tell me all of your ideas." I playfully smacked her butt and walked to the closet.

"Keith," Donna called my name just as I opened the closet door.

I started to answer, but stopped cold when I saw the inside of the closet. Donna walked up behind me and placed her arms around my waist.

"I meant to tell you about the closet," she said with sheepish look on her face.

The closet was like something out of a magazine. Everything was perfectly coordinated, with the pants hanging on the bottom half, shirts on top, shoes lined up neatly, and sweaters folded flat. The only problem I could find, or, should I say, couldn't find, was my clothes. I turned to Donna.

"Where are my clothes?"

"Well, you know how there wasn't enough room in the closet with all of our things right?"

I nodded.

"Well, I figured I could put your clothes in the closet in the guest bedroom. That way we could have our own space. You don't mind, do you?"

"Why didn't you put your clothes in the guest room?" I asked, trying my best to remain calm.

"Because I have more clothes than you." She put her arms back around me and laid her head on my chest. "I thought we could do it this way until we moved into someplace bigger."

"Donna, you could have at least let me know or asked me before making these kinds of changes. I don't want to walk to another room to get dressed."

She pulled away from me. "So, I can't do anything in *your* house without asking permission? When I moved in here you said to make myself at home, and, after the wedding, this will be my home too. So, if something has changed, let me know now because if I'm going to be treated like a child, I would rather live in my mother's house."

I could see where the conversation was heading, so I tried to smooth things over. "No, baby, I want you to make yourself at home. I told you before that I would leave the decorating up to you, and I meant that. I was just surprised when I saw all of my things were moved. It felt kind of like you were trying to get rid of me already." I smiled weakly.

"I can put everything back if you want. I thought you would appreciate it because the closet was so cluttered."

She moved towards the closet and began pulling her blouses off of the hangers.

"No, it's fine and it does look better," I said, taking the clothes out of her hands and placing them back on the wooden hangers.

"Thank you," she hugged me tight.

"And, anyway, I know damn well you don't want to live with your mother," I whispered in her ear.

"Whatever. Just try me," she said before kissing my neck.

I walked down the hall silently praying for God to give me strength to deal with Donna and her selfish behavior. Sometimes I had to wonder if she really appreciated me and all of the things I have done for her. It didn't take me long to realize that Donna is selfish and very opportunistic, but despite all of that, like a fool, I still wanted her to be my wife. I also realized that there are very few sisters out here who would still have me knowing that I also like men, so I figured it was a win-win situation.

I walked past the guest bedroom that now housed my clothes and walked downstairs instead. I made myself a sandwich to hold me over until dinner and sat down to watch some television. I was cracking up laughing, watching one of my favorite movies *Stir Crazy*, with Richard Pryor and Gene Wilder, when the phone in the kitchen rang. I got up to answer it but it stopped mid-ring. I heard Donna on the phone upstairs, so I sat back down to enjoy the movie. Just as Richard Pryor started saying, "We bad, we bad," my cell phone rang. I ignored the call and continued watching the movie. My cell started ringing non-stop. Donna came into the living room and grabbed my cell just as I was getting up to turn it off.

"Aren't you going to answer your phone?" she asked while looking at the caller ID.

"Nah, whoever it is can wait. I'm chilling right now. You can turn it off."

"I think you should answer it," she said, holding the phone out to me.

From the look on her face, I thought it might be Jarrod on the other end of the phone. I quickly dispelled that idea once I remembered he didn't have my new number. I took the phone from her hand, looked at the caller ID and inwardly screamed. Donna stood over top of me with her arms crossed, almost daring me not to answer.

"She knows you're here, Keith. I just talked to her on the phone and told her to call your cell. I promised her that I would make sure you answered this time. Answer it."

I took a deep breath and answered, "Hello?"

"Hi, Keith. It's Jackie."

"Hey, Jackie. How are you?"

Donna sat down next to me and leaned in to hear the conversation.

"If I didn't know any better, I would think you were avoiding me," Jackie said lightly.

"No, I've just been busy. I'm sorry I haven't gotten back to you. I was actually planning on calling you later in the week," I lied.

"No problem. Keith. I know Donna told you that I spoke to her, and she told me some things that were quite disturbing."

I glanced at Donna. "Yeah, she told me."

"Is it true?" Jackie sounded like she was crying.

I was silent.

"Keith? Please tell me. I need to know."

At that very moment, I wished I was anywhere and doing anything else but sitting in my living room telling my old friend that her husband is bisexual and we had been intimate.

"Jackie, whatever Donna told you is true. I'm sorry."

I heard Jackie weeping on the other end of the phone, and I felt horrible. It was as though I were personally responsible for her pain, even more so than Jarrod in a way. Jackie was my friend before Jarrod, and my loyalty should have remained with her. But when I introduced the two of them, I never let her know for fear that I would expose myself.

"I need to hear it from you Keith. I want, no I need, to know everything.

Donna tapped my arm and mouthed, "Tell her."

The only sound to be heard while I told Jackie the story of how Jarrod and I got together was the sound of her sniffing and blowing her nose. When I finished, it felt as though a great burden had been lifted from my shoulders.

"So, are you saying my husband likes to be fucked in the ass? Are you telling me Jarrod has kissed me with the same lips that have sucked another man's dick?" She was becoming angrier with every question.

I was silent.

Jackie asked me several more unintelligible questions through her sobs. Several minutes later, she calmed down enough to continue her interrogation.

"Keith, you said you and Jarrod got together in our sophomore year, right?"

I hated the way she said, "got together." I didn't see it that way, since I didn't really participate.

"Yeah."

"But you introduced us that year. So did y'all do it before or after you introduced us?"

"Before," I said it as softly as I could.

"Excuse me?" she yelled in my ear.

"Before," I said louder.

"You are sick! How could you do that? Thanks, *friend*!"

I wished I could disappear. "I'm sorry, Jackie. We were young, and I really didn't mean to hurt you."

"So were you the only one? Or have there been more?"

I could name at least ten men and maybe twice as many women off the top of my head that Jarrod had been with since I introduced the two of them. I was sure she would die if she knew that he was freaking the pastor that married them, but I didn't feel right telling this to her.

"Jackie, I really don't mind telling you about anything to

do with me and Jarrod, because I owe you that much, but I really think you need to talk to Jarrod about everything else."

"Hell, no! You owe me an answer to every question I ask you. It's the very least you should do. Now, I need to know, were you the only one?"

I looked at Donna who was still staring at me with a hint of amusement in her eyes. She looked like she could have been getting some sort of sick pleasure out of seeing me squirm. I could have choked her. Here she was being so righteous by allowing Jackie to put me on the spot, and she probably didn't even tell her about seeing Jarrod out with Sabrina.

I decided to tell Jackie what she really didn't want to know. "No, Jackie, I wasn't the only one."

I had to pull the phone away from my ear because of the screaming. Once Jackie calmed down, I heard the sound of a baby crying in the distance.

"Keith, I have to go. I don't know if I should say thank you or not. Thanks for being honest, but I will never forgive you for not having my best interest at heart when you should have." With that, she hung up in my ear.

Donna looked at me expectantly, "What did she say?" she asked.

I put the phone down and walked upstairs, ignoring Donna as she shouted my name.

For the rest of the weekend, I barely said two words to Donna, because she still saw nothing wrong with her telling Jackie my business. She tried to get back into my good graces on Tuesday night by cooking my favorite meal of barbeque chicken, macaroni and cheese, and cabbage, but when that didn't work she tried other tactics. Each morning before work, I would wake up to a hot breakfast, and she would even pack a lunch for me. I was dumbfounded, because any other time I couldn't pay Donna to cook. By the time Thursday rolled around I had begun to calm down, but I had to admit, it was nice to have Donna going out of her way to please me for a change, so I kept up the silent treatment. On Friday after work, Donna was waiting for me in the parking lot. When I saw her, I smiled to myself and casually walked to her.

"Hey," I said.

"Hey, yourself," she reached for me and pulled me into a kiss. "Keith, I don't like it when we are like this. I miss talking to you. I miss you holding me, and more than anything, I miss feeling you inside of me." She nibbled on my earlobe and massaged the hardness in my crotch. "Can we go back to how we were?"

"And how's that?" I asked in a low voice. My breathing became heavy, and I held back a moan.

"You've hardly talked to me or touched me all week, and I miss you." She was trying to put on a pout, and it was all I could do not to crack a smile. She must have seen me breaking, because she went in for the kill by putting my hands up her skirt and grinding against my fingers. When I felt that she wasn't wearing any panties, I couldn't fight it anymore, and I pushed her against my truck and kissed her deeply. I've always been sort of an exhibitionist, so the fact that we were outside in broad daylight and possibly being watched turned me on. I was so into it that I didn't notice that we *were* being watched. Only, the person watching us was not who I had in mind.

"I've been told that there are a couple of cheap motels over on City Avenue that rent rooms by the hour," my father said loudly.

Donna and I jumped up like two teenagers who had been caught in the act. Donna straightened her skirt while I adjusted my pants to hide my erection.

"Hello, Mr. Reed," Donna said.

"Hey, Dad. I didn't see you coming," I said.

"I guess not. I think you two should take this show on the road. Anybody could have seen you. Luckily, it was only me." His eyes traveled from me to Donna.

I noticed that his eyes seemed to linger on Donna's erect nipples, which were very pronounced in her silk blouse, a few seconds longer than necessary.

Donna noticed too and wrapped her arms around herself, "Keith, I can meet you at the house. Nice seeing you, Mr. Reed." She stumbled and nearly fell while trying to rush to her car.

My father barely acknowledged her with a nod. I helped her to steady herself and walked her the rest of the way to her car. We shared a few kisses before she finally pulled away. I stood there watching her car drive away, wishing I were with her. The last thing I wanted to do was have my father chastise me like I was still a mischievous teenager.

I took my time returning to where my father stood with a smug look on his face. "So what's up, Dad?"

"I should be asking you the same question. I know you have more sense than to dry hump your girlfriend in broad daylight for all the world to see."

"Dad, please. I am a grown man, and we were just having a little fun." I laughed.

"You're right, you are grown, but you also need to act like it. There is a time and place for everything. And say what you want about me, but you've never seen me carry on like that in public. It's tacky." He had the nerve to look disappointed. "It's bad enough you feel the need to marry that hoodrat, but now you are letting her bring you down to her level."

"Her level? And what's that supposed to mean? She is more woman than any of the *women* you've been with."

"Your mother would turn over in her grave if she saw who you've chosen to make your wife and bring into this family. I don't understand you. Any woman would give her right arm to be with you. You can do better, Keith," he said.

"You know what, Dad? I will not have this conversation with you. If I need an opinion about what type of woman I should be with, trust me when I say that you would be the very last person I would consult. Marrying my mother was the best thing you've ever done, and none of your so-called women are qualified to even scrub her floors."

I turned away from his angry glare to get in my truck and leave before things got even uglier. As I backed out of my parking space, I stopped next to him and rolled down the window.

"And for the record, you don't show public displays of affection with your women, not because it's tacky, it's because you can't. All of your affairs *have* to be conducted behind closed doors because you *can't* be seen in public. Now, that's tacky. In the meantime, I'm going to do what makes me happy, and if you or anybody else has a problem with it, then that's just too damn bad."

I turned up the music loud enough to drown out my father's retort and sped out of the parking lot.

Donna met me at the front door wearing nothing but a smile, so I carried her upstairs and showed her just how much I missed her. Donna suggested that we go to Warmdaddy's, a restaurant in South Philly, to get some of their famous cornmeal fried catfish and listen to some jazz. During the drive, Donna and I discussed the situation about Jackie and Jarrod.

"Keith, I feel like it's only fair that Jackie know the truth about Jarrod. But I do want to apologize for putting you on the spot. I didn't know you would react the way you did," she said.

"Yeah, I was pissed, and truth be told, I'm still hot over that."

"I know, but don't you think she had a right to know? I mean, her husband is screwing men, not to mention, he was just all up in Sabrina's face."

"I feel where you are coming from, Donna, but, in any case, I should have been your first concern. We are going to be married soon, and I need to know you have my back. I don't want to feel like you are going to put me out on Front Street the next time you need to prove a point. You know what I mean?" I took my eyes off the road for a moment to look at her. "And while you were on this whole girl power trip, I'm willing to bet you failed to mention to her about Jarrod being with Sabrina."

She looked at me and said nothing.

"Well, did you tell her?"

She looked sad, and I wanted to feel sorry for her, but I was happy that she was finally feeling the heat.

"No, I didn't tell her."

"Why not?"

She hesitated for a moment, and I knew I had her right where I wanted her.

"Because...I don't know, Keith. Well..." She was stuck.

"I know why. Because Sabrina is your girl, that's why. Now, how am I supposed to feel about that? You would rather protect a fake-ass, jealous-hearted, so-called friend than your man. I would never do that to you, and you know it. That was fucked up, Donna."

"I know, Keith," she whispered. "I never really thought about it like that."

Her head hung low and I saw that she was really feeling bad. I didn't want another discussion about Jarrod and Jackie to ruin our evening, so I tried to lighten the mood.

"Now she knows my business, and I'm wondering if she is going to go on a man-hating rampage and spread my business. Jackie will probably take out an ad in the *Daily News*. I can see it now. My picture will be on the front page, and the headline will read: 'Watch Out Ladies, He'll Take Your Man!'"

Donna chuckled and wiped the tears that had been form-ing in her eyes, "I'm sorry, baby. I was wrong, and you have every right to feel the way you do. I promise it won't happen again."

"What?" I said in mock surprise, "Did you just say you're wrong? I don't believe it. Let me write this down on my calendar so I can remember this. God only knows the next time I'll ever hear those words again."

She punched my arm playfully. "Cut it out, I do admit when I'm wrong. It's not my fault that I'm usually right." We both laughed.

We walked into the restaurant hand-in-hand and were seated almost immediately. Once we ordered our drinks, hers a Strawberry Mojito and mine a Daddy Long Leggs Lemonade, we settled in and listened to the live jazz band. We grooved to the music as we ate our food. Donna suggested that we order several of our favorite entrees so we wouldn't miss out on anything. After grubbing on some fried catfish, barbeque short ribs, Southern fried chicken, garlic mashed potatoes, and smoked turkey collard greens, we were feeling no pain.

"All of that work I've been putting in at the gym lately has flown out of the window," I laughed.

"You know you still look good boy, so stop trippin'." She reached over and massaged my chest.

"I do, don't I?" I said as I stroked my chin.

She laughed. "I think you've had too much to drink."

"Come on now, I'm just getting started. What, you can't hang?" I asked as I signaled our waitress to bring us another round. "If you scared, say you scared."

"Don't even try it. You know the one good thing I inherited from my mother is a wooden leg. Shit, you know what it is. I can drink your ass under the table any day of the week. Come on, bring it on, baby, man up!"

One of the things I love most about Donna is that I can have just as much fun with her as I do with my boys. She can talk shit with the best of them and even back it up. And she was right, she can drink me under the table, something she has proven time and time again.

"Damn," I said as I reached in my wallet.

"What's wrong?"

"I keep forgetting about the AIDS fundraiser. I have to get rid of these tickets, and I only have a few weeks to sell them. Otherwise, I'll have to buy them myself."

"You need any help?" she asked.

"Actually, I do. Thanks for the offer. Do you think you can take some to your job? And maybe you can sell some at the new salon you go to. From what I've heard about some of the women in there, I'm sure they could use all of the AIDS pamphlets they can get."

Donna put down her drink, "And what exactly have you heard?"

"Let's put it this way, I've heard a whole lot. Men talk, baby, just as much as y'all do."

"I ain't even mad at you, because you are probably right." We fell out laughing.

"Speaking of the salon." She smoothed her hair down. "I need to call Sheena tomorrow and see if she can squeeze me in.

My hair is looking tore up. I love how my hair looks when she does it, but it's just so hard to get an appointment."

"Why didn't you make an appointment the last time you were in there?"

"Because I'm so used to being able to just pop in on Sabrina, and now I have to get used to doing it the right way. I have to admit, Sabrina gets on my damn nerves, but having her do my hair was convenient."

I nodded my head toward the front of the restaurant where several people were waiting to be seated. "Speak of the devil."

"Huh?" Donna turned around to see what I was talking about.

Sabrina was standing in the doorway looking outside as though she was waiting for someone. Donna sucked her teeth and turned back around. "Oh God, I do not feel like dealing with her tonight," she said.

"Why would you need to deal with her? We are having a great time, so don't let her ruin your night. She might not even see you."

"You're right. Let's get some dessert to go. I want to get you home so we can finish what we started earlier." She reached under the table and teased me by playing with my zipper.

I winked at her then waved to our waitress and ordered sweet potato cheese cake and bread pudding to go. While I tried to focus on anything but Donna's hand trying to undo my zipper, my eyes roamed back over to where Sabrina was standing. My heart skipped a beat when I saw whom Sabrina was now talking to. Jarrod stood next to her with his arm slung casually around her waist. I inhaled deeply and let out a low moan. Donna, who must have thought I was responding to her advances, smiled and tried even harder to work on my zipper.

"Let's get out of here," I said, hoping that Jarrod and Sabrina would be seated without Donna spotting Jarrod. The last thing I needed was for Donna to see him and get an attitude. I moved Donna's hand and moved to her side of the table, putting my back to the front door.

"What's the hurry? We haven't gotten our dessert yet." She gave up on my zipper but kept on rubbing. "We can't leave, anyway. She didn't give us the check yet."

"I'll just leave enough on the table to cover the bill and her tip." I looked over my shoulder to keep one eye on Sabrina and Jarrod, who so far hadn't looked our way. "It's taking too long. We can pick something up on the way home."

She looked around the restaurant for our waitress, and I prayed she wouldn't look near the door. "I know what your problem is. You just want to get me home so you can get some. Uh huh, you ain't slick." She smiled at me seductively. "Alright, well, let me use the bathroom first, because these drinks are running through me. If the waitress is not here by the time I get back, we can go, okay?"

I nodded my head, and she got up to find the bathroom. When the waitress finally returned with our dessert, I asked her to bring our check. Donna was making her way back over to the table when I felt a tap on my shoulder.

"What's up, Keith?" I turned around to see Jarrod and

Sabrina now standing behind me. "We were waiting to be seated when I saw you sitting over here."

"Hey, Jarrod. How are you, Sabrina?" She rolled her eyes and moved closer to Jarrod.

When Donna reached the table, she glared at me with her eyes full of questions.

"Hey, baby. Jarrod and Sabrina just came over to say hello," I said as I reached for her to sit next to me. Donna did not acknowledge either of them.

"So what do you say we sit with you guys?" Jarrod asked, reaching for a chair. "Otherwise we'll be waiting all night for a table. What do you think?"

Jarrod did not take his eyes off my face the entire time he'd been standing there.

"We were actually just about to leave. We're waiting for the waitress to—" I started before Donna cut in.

"Just say no!" she hissed. "Fuck it, I'll say it. Hell, no, you can't join us," she said, looking at Jarrod for the first time.

I shook my head, because I knew this was going to turn ugly at any moment.

Jarrod smiled tightly. "First of all, I wasn't talking to you. I was talking to my *boy,* Keith."

Sabrina sucked her teeth and said, "Come on, Jarrod, you don't need to be begging them for nothing. And I don't really want to sit with this fake-ass bitch anyway."

"Bitch?" Donna said while rising from her seat. I pulled her back down, because a few of the other patrons were beginning to take notice.

"Yeah, *bitch.* I didn't stutter. Don't nobody want to be with your tired ass, anyway. You just jealous, anyway."

"Jealous of what? The fact that once again you got a man who's going to dog you out?" Donna said.

"No, because ever since you got with Keith, you act like you better than everybody else, and it just kills you to see me with somebody with money."

Jarrod stood next to Sabrina and smiled at me.

"Don't forget, I knew you before he came along," Sabrina continued. "You ain't have shit then, and if it wasn't for him," she said, pointing at me, "you still wouldn't have shit. You broke, with a bullshit job and ain't got nothing going for you, but your man. So instead of you worrying about who you think is going to dog me out, you better pray that *your man* don't leave your ass high and dry."

People were now definitely starting to take notice of the confrontation, and I saw a woman who I assumed was the manager approaching our table.

"Shit," I said. I looked at Jarrod, who was still staring at me. "I think y'all need to leave. Jarrod, please take your friend and go."

Donna moved forward, and, as hard as I tried, I could not get her to sit back down.

"No, fuck that. She said what she had to say, so now it's my turn. First of all, he's not your man, because he's somebody's husband, you nasty trick. And secondly, I don't think I'm better than you. *You* think I'm better than you. Shit, you're one client away from losing everything, you miserable bitch."

Sabrina laughed and looked directly at me before saying, "Now, ain't that the trick-ass pot calling the kettle black. Yeah, he's somebody's husband, for now, but so is your boss. So before you throw stones, think about it before some of them bones start falling out of your closet."

Donna took another step forward, and I stepped in between the two angry women before their flying words turned into flying fists and hair-pulling. I was sure my baby could hold her own, but Sabrina was a big girl, and I didn't know if Donna would make it out on top in a brawl with her.

The manager, who was now trailed by a tall, heavyset brother, stepped in and asked, "Is everything all right over here?" She smiled tightly, but her professional demeanor remained intact. "Yes, we were just leaving," I said. I left enough money on the table to cover the bill and a healthy tip for our waitress. Donna and Sabrina were staring each other down, waiting to pounce on each other. I took our coats and led Donna away from the table and toward the door.

"Talk to you later, Keith," Jarrod said to my back.

Donna turned to me after we made it outside, and I helped her with her coat, "I can't stand that bitch! I should've whipped her ass."

"She is not worth the trouble, baby. You are better than that," I said as I opened the door and let her in the truck.

Donna spent the majority of the ride home fussing and cussing about Sabrina. I only half-listened to what she was saying because my mind was on Jarrod. If I had known then what I know now, I would have never given into him. He was as bad as, if not worse than, a scorned woman. He was deliberately going out of his way to cause problems for me. A small part of me was worried that, out of anger, he would tell my secret. But I knew Jarrod couldn't tell on me without telling on himself, and I was certain he would never share his double-life with anyone. Then Sabrina's last words hit me like a ton of bricks. Just as I was going to question Donna about what Sabrina meant about her boss being married, she shouted in my ear.

"Keith, did you hear me?"

"Huh? I'm sorry, baby. I don't know where my head is. What did you say?"

I kept my eyes on the road, but my mind was still focused on the meaning behind Sabrina's statement.

"Yeah, well, your mind better not have been on that flame-ass, Jarrod. What the hell did he mean, he'll talk to you later?"

"I have no idea, Donna. I told him at the luncheon not to call me anymore, and you know he hasn't been calling me because you would've known."

"I don't know shit. Yeah, he ain't calling the house, but how do I know he's not calling you at the office or on your cell?"

"Donna, I haven't seen or talked to Jarrod since the luncheon." I looked at her to see her reaction.

"The luncheon? And what did y'all talk about?"

"Nothing. I told him it would be best if we didn't associate anymore." I chose my words carefully.

"That's your damn problem. You're too damn nice. Why can't you just tell him to leave you and me the fuck alone?" I saw our perfect night going up in flames right before my eyes.

"Donna, what more can I do? It's not my fault he's acting this way. I have done everything you've asked. So you tell me, what else can I do?" I parked in front of the house and turned to face her.

"Don't ask me. You started it, now you fix it, Keith. Do whatever you have to do because I'm not going to keep worrying about you and him." Her eyes were wet with tears and her voice was beginning to crack.

"I'll tell you what, after this fundraiser, I will resign from the league. That way there will be absolutely no reason for me to associate with him. How's that sound?"

She sighed deeply and nodded her head. "I hope you're right, Keith. I would hate to have to leave you, but I will if this continues. I need to feel secure in my relationships, and right now, I don't feel very secure."

I hesitated to ask her about Sabrina's words because I knew she was already upset, but I needed to know, "Donna, what was Sabrina talking about back there? You know, about your boss?"

She stayed quiet longer than necessary, and then finally said, "Why are you trying to change the subject?"

"Because I want to know, is there something I should know about you and your boss?"

She gave me my answer by not answering right away. "She was just trying to start trouble. Don't pay her any mind."

I looked at her and decided not to push the issue, because I didn't think I really wanted to know the truth. The thought of her sleeping with some white man was probably more sickening to me than finding me in my situation was for her. I guess what goes around, comes around.

Neither of us was in the mood for anything other than sleep after the night we had, so we said our good nights and slept as far apart as possible.

JACKIE
AND
JARROD

After Keith and Donna left the restaurant, the manager insisted that Jarrod and Sabrina leave as well. Jarrod was able to convince the manager that the scene between Sabrina and Donna had only been a misunderstanding and promised that there would not be any more trouble. The manager relented, and they were seated a short time later.

Jarrod was upset that once again Keith acted as though he didn't exist. In his mind, Donna was the only thing standing in his way of finally getting Keith right where he wanted him. Over the past few weeks, he'd become consumed with anger over Keith's rejection and decided he would gladly leave his wife and child if Keith would have him. As far as he knew, no one outside of a few select members of the league and Donna knew about the other side of Keith. Once he found out that Sabrina and Donna had been friends, he started to pick her brain for information about Donna and Keith's relationship, and, from what he could gather,

Donna had made no mention to Sabrina of finding out that Keith was bisexual. Jarrod figured that the perfect way to get Donna out of the picture once and for all would be to embarrass her. He decided that's where Sabrina would come in. When Jarrod met Sabrina in the club, he correctly figured her to be good for a quick and easy fuck. But after she relayed the information to him about the exchange between her and Donna and he saw that she disliked Donna almost as much as he did, he decided to keep her around for a while. Jarrod looked across the table at Sabrina, who was trying her best to act classy. He laughed to himself, because he actually felt sorry for her, because she really believed he would leave his wife and let her into his world. Jarrod told Sabrina that she was the type of woman he wished his wife was, and she ate it up. He knew how women like Sabrina operated, thinking freaky sex would turn him out enough to keep him coming back for more and eventually make an honest woman out of her. What a joke. Granted, sex with Sabrina was good, but she could never give him what he craved the most, a strong, hard, male body. So, for the time being he would allow Sabrina to think he would be her meal ticket, and he would let her serve her purpose, to get rid of Donna.

After ordering their drinks, Jarrod looked at the menu and asked, "What are you in the mood for tonight?"

She tried unsuccessfully to bat her eyes, only to wind up looking like a fool. "Um, do they have chicken fingers?"

"How about I order for you?"

"That sounds good," Sabrina said as she looked around and took in her surroundings. She wanted to remember every detail of the restaurant, because she couldn't be sure when she would return. Sabrina was excited at the prospect of her and Jarrod becoming serious and having a relationship. She wondered how she could have gotten so lucky to have found a man like Jarrod, who wanted to get to know her and take her out on a real date. The men Sabrina was used to dealing with had no idea how to treat a woman. Their idea of a date was takeout from the corner Chinese store and freaky sex.

"I was glad you called me, Jarrod. I didn't think I would hear from you anymore."

Jarrod wasn't in the mood for small talk, so he ignored her statement and decided to cut to the chase.

"So what's up with you and Donna? I thought you said that was your girl."

"No, I said she used to be my girl."

"What happened?"

"Like I said before, she's fake. Remember how I told you she was acting the night we met? Flipping out and shit because she knows about your wife?"

Jarrod nodded.

"That's how she's been acting ever since she got back with Keith, like she's on this holier-than-thou kick. She's forgetting that before Keith and, hell, even after she got with him, she messed around with married men. And now she's all up in my business, trying to tell me right from wrong."

"Yeah, Keith is pretty much the same way. He has a few secrets of his own that I'm sure he would like to keep hidden, which is why he was acting so shady tonight."

Just like Jarrod planned, Sabrina took the bait, and her ears immediately perked up at the thought of trouble in Donna's perfect world.

"Yeah, I was wondering about that. What's up with him?" she asked.

When the waitress came to take their order, Jarrod chose crab cakes for him and jumbo shrimp for her. He waved the waitress away, anxious to get on with his story.

Jarrod cleared his throat. "I don't know if I told you, but me and Keith were roommates in college, and when you are that close to someone all the time, you get to see the real person."

Jarrod paused long enough to tailor the story to his liking, but not so long as to make Sabrina think it was false.

"I started noticing how he would look at me when he thought I wasn't paying attention. I would just brush it off, thinking I was tripping, you know?" Sabrina nodded. "He used to talk about homosexuals, especially men, like he hated them or something, and you know what they say about men who do that. Well, one night after we came in from partying." Jarrod paused and looked directly into Sabrina's eyes. "Do me a favor, please don't tell anyone what I'm about to tell you. I still consider Keith a good friend, and I don't want any of this to get out, because it could ruin him. Not to mention what it could do to his and Donna's relationship. You get what I'm saying?"

Sabrina looked as though she was ready to burst with excitement. "I promise, I won't say a word to anyone."

"Ok, so, after the party, we came in, and I fell asleep.

Next thing I knew, I woke up and Keith was trying to get into bed with me. At first, I thought he was just drunk and didn't know what he was doing, so I pushed him away from me and told him to get the hell out of my bed. But then he started talking about how he was attracted to me and asking me to let him touch me."

Jarrod looked away from Sabrina, trying to look embarrassed by his revelation.

"So what did you do?" Sabrina asked scooting closer.

"What do you think I did? I kicked his ass out of my bed and told him if he ever tried that shit again, I would fuck him up."

Sabrina looked at Jarrod in disbelief, "And you're still friends with him? That's crazy. I don't know any man who would stay friends with somebody after that went down."

"I tried to get another roommate, but I couldn't, so I just kept my distance for a while. He never tried anything else after that, and eventually we started hanging out again. But, trust me, I slept with one eye open. You wanna know what's really crazy? He always had a bunch of women, and I didn't see or hear about him with any men until our senior year. I went home for Spring Break, but Keith didn't want to go home, because his mother had just passed away and he didn't really get along with his father. So I came back a day early, and when I tried to get into the room, Keith was acting all shady, blocking the door and trying to get me to leave and come back later. I thought he was in there with a woman or something, so I started joking with him and trying to figure out who it was. He started getting real agitated and nervous, and that made me even more curious, so I pushed the door open."

Jarrod stopped talking because the waitress arrived with their food. He dug into his food, ignoring Sabrina's angry glare

"I'm going to eat my food while it's hot, and I suggest you do the same."

Sabrina picked up her fork, and they ate in silence. When Jarrod was done, he picked up the story where he left off.

"When I opened the door, Keith was standing there naked and holding a shirt to cover himself." Jarrod paused to take a sip of his drink and buy himself some time to come up with a surprise ending to his story.

Sabrina was beyond excited. "Who was he with? Don't tell me it was a man!"

Jarrod nodded slowly. "Better than that, it was *the* man. The R.A."

Sabrina look confused. "The who?"

Jarrod sighed. "The R.A., you know, resident advisor? Well, he was also the head of the basketball team, and there he was, fumbling with his pants, trying to hide in the closet." Jarrod laughed at the pun.

"Get the fuck outta here!" Sabrina shouted.

"Shhh!" Jarrod looked around, embarrassed at once again being the center of attention. He couldn't wait until he could be done with her.

"He was fucking another dude?" Sabrina whispered. She started laughing uncontrollably, and Jarrod was sure his mission had been accomplished.

"What did you do?" she asked.

"What could I do? Keith started trying to explain, and I

just left the room. Since we only had a couple of months left until graduation, we stayed roommates. But after we graduated, we went our separate ways until we ran into each other a few years ago. We were cool for a while, but I think once he got with Donna, he started to distance himself from me because I know how he really gets down."

Sabrina giggled. "I wonder what Ms. Perfect would say if she knew her man was a homo."

Jarrod tried to contain his smile. "Sabrina, I thought I asked you not to say anything. What I told you has to stay between us. I'm trusting you. If we are going to be together, I need to be able to confide in you."

"Oh, no. I'm not going to say anything. Shit, that's what she gets."

"I told you that because I can see how she could be jealous of you."

He ran his thumb across Sabrina's cheek. Flattered by his compliment, Sabrina blushed deeply.

Jarrod went in for the kill. "I just thought it was something you should know, because I don't want you to think she has something special. So the next time she tries to throw something in your face, just think about Keith and his secret. Donna isn't any better than you. In fact, I think you came out on top. I'm your man now, and at least you won't have to worry about me creeping with any men."

Sabrina was bursting at the seams at the thought of being able to call Jarrod her man. She couldn't believe her luck and wondered how the night could get any more perfect.

Jarrod spent the rest of the evening with a smile on his face, confident that it would be only a matter of time before Sabrina ran her mouth about Keith.

After dinner, Sabrina suggested they go back to her place for a nightcap. Jarrod knew it was too late to call on the pastor, so he readily agreed. When Jarrod asked Sabrina to try anal sex, a first for them, he was ecstatic when she answered by stripping and bending over. It was Jarrod's turn to be excited, because he couldn't believe his good fortune when she allowed him to fuck her without any mention of protection.

*　　*　　*

Jackie looked at the clock again as she tried to soothe her crying daughter. She had decided that this would be the day she would confront Jarrod about his sexuality. After Keith confirmed what Donna told her, she knew she needed to get out of the marriage fast. Although she wished she could be home with Naomi and enjoy being a stay-at-home mother, Jackie knew she would have to go back to work once she was on her own. In a moment of insanity, she had even thought of staying with Jarrod and continuing to be a family, but common sense prevailed, and she made her decision. She would ask Jarrod to leave. With child support, alimony, and her savings, Jackie figured she could stay home for a little over a year. She thought back to all of those times she wished Jarrod would make love to her and thanked God he hadn't. Who knew what diseases he picked up, she thought? Over the last two weeks, Jackie had tried several times to talk to Jarrod, but whenever he came home from work, if he came home at all, he would walk right by her and the baby without so much as a single word.

She had called Jarrod at 8:00, which was over two hours ago, to tell him to get home right away, because she had some things she needed to discuss with him. Surprisingly, he said he would be home soon, but, as usual, he left her hanging. Since Naomi, their six-week-old daughter, had been born, Jarrod had been spending more and more time away from home. Foolishly, Jackie thought that once the baby was born, Jarrod would come to his senses and fall in love with their baby girl as much as she did, but he paid neither of them any mind.

When Jackie heard Jarrod's key in the front door, she put the now-quiet baby down, and walked into the foyer. Jarrod swung the door open and staggered into the house.

"Have you been drinking?" Jackie asked, taking a step back.

Jarrod pushed past her and walked up the stairs to their bedroom. Jackie went to pick Naomi up and followed behind him.

She sighed. "Jarrod, I need to talk to you."

He ignored her and walked into the bathroom. Jackie placed Naomi in the bassinet and stood in the doorway of the bathroom.

"Jarrod…"

"Can't you see I'm busy?" he said before slamming the door in her face.

Jackie paced in front of the door, trying to figure out exactly what she wanted to say to Jarrod.

"Jarrod, I'm not leaving until you come out. We need to talk."

She heard the toilet flush and then the bathroom door swung open. Jarrod stood there with his pants undone and a maniacal look on his face.

"Talk about what?" he said as he walked closer to her. "You always need to talk about something. I'm tired of talking, how about you shut up for once and put your mouth to better use." Jarrod backed her onto the bed and pulled his pants down. He pushed her on the bed and kissed her forcefully.

Jackie struggled to get up. "Jarrod, what are you doing?"

"What's the problem? Isn't this what you wanted?" he slurred.

"No, I want to talk to you about something very important." Jackie tried to move away from Jarrod. He had a tendency to be nasty when he drank, which wasn't too often, but she always tried to steer clear of him when he had too much to drink.

"Fuck talking." He moved toward her once more. "I want sex."

"Jarrod, not right now, please."

Jarrod blocked her path and pushed her back on the bed.

"Not right now? What, you fuckin' somebody else or something?" he asked as he stood over top of her.

"No, of course not."

"So what's the problem?"

"Nothing, but you haven't tried to touch me in months, and now you are all over me. I'm just surprised is all."

"Look, either I can take it, or you can give it to me. Which one is it?" Jarrod asked as he stroked himself.

"Wait."

"Fuck it!" Jarrod reached under Jackie's nightgown and pulled at her panties.

Jackie tried her best to struggle against Jarrod's advances, but he was too strong for her. His wet, sloppy kisses made her want to vomit. When Jackie felt her panties rip and Jarrod's fingers digging into her skin, she screamed.

"Jarrod, please stop. You're scaring me!"

"I thought you liked it rough," he growled in her ear.

Jackie knew that at any moment, Jarrod would enter her and she knew she had to act quickly.

"Jarrod, if you want to have sex, we can, but you need to use a condom."

Jarrod froze. "What the fuck you mean I gotta use a condom? You are fucking somebody aren't you?" He pushed himself off of her and pulled his pants back on.

Jackie sat up and tried to cover herself. "No, Jarrod, I'm not."

"Bitch, don't lie to me. Who you fucking? My wife tells me I need to use a condom, and I'm supposed to believe she ain't fucking nobody?"

Jackie was getting frightened, "Jarrod, please, the baby," she said motioning toward the still-sleeping Naomi.

Jarrod ignored her request and asked, "So, who are you fucking? I know if you ain't fuckin' me, you fuckin' somebody, so who is it?"

"Nobody. I asked you to wear the condom because I know you're sleeping with someone else."

"You don't know shit. And if I was, could you blame me? Look at you. You let yourself go and you're getting fat."

Jackie's fear was replaced with anger. "Fat? I just had your child, and you have the nerve to call me fat?"

"Nobody told you to get pregnant." He paused, "Is that my baby, or is it the other guy's?"

What he said hit her like a slap in the face. "I can't believe you just asked me that. I should be asking you who you're fucking." She stood up. "So who are you fucking? Huh, Jarrod? What's *his* name?"

Jarrod was struck silent as he absorbed what she said to him.

"What did you say to me?"

Jackie regained her confidence and said, "You heard me. What's his name? Oh what, you think I didn't know? I know all about it. Here I was thinking you were sleeping around with women. Boy, was I wrong."

"Shut up, Jackie," Jarrod said quietly.

He'd often thought about what would happen if Jackie ever found out about his sexuality. He thought he would enjoy telling her how she wasn't enough to satisfy him. His plan was to get Keith, then break the news to Jackie and watch her break down. He knew she would wonder if it was something she did that would make her husband leave her for, of all things, a man. But she did know, and she was throwing it in his face. Jarrod racked his brain trying to figure out how she could have found out.

For the first time in years, Jackie was standing up to Jarrod, and it felt damn good. She moved closer to him and pointed her finger in his face.

"No, you shut the fuck up. I've been hearing some very interesting things about you lately and it sickens me."

Her eyes began to fill with tears. Their yelling woke the baby, who was now beginning to whimper.

"Who told you that?"

"Does it matter? But if you must know, I talked to Donna, Keith's girlfriend, and she told me everything. And I mean everything, Jarrod," Jackie said as she rubbed Naomi's back to quiet her down.

"What the fuck were you doing talking to her?" Jarrod yelled.

He couldn't believe that bitch was once again interfering with his life.

"I called Keith's house trying to find who you were talking to every night, and when she answered, I thought she was the one you were creeping with. But then she told me how she found you and Keith together. Jarrod how could you do this to me? A man, Jarrod? It's no use in denying it either because I talked to Keith too, and he admitted it."

Jackie could no longer hold back the tears, and she broke into quiet sobs.

The bedroom was quiet except for the sound of Naomi's

whimpering and Jarrod's heavy footsteps as he paced the floor. Jackie picked the baby up and held her in her arms.

Once she was asleep, Jackie walked slowly to the nursery to lay her down in the crib. Through her tears, Jackie stared at Naomi for a few moments, careful not to let any of her tears fall on the sleeping baby's face.

"I love you, Naomi," she whispered. She felt as though her whole world were falling apart.

When Jackie returned to her bedroom, she stood in the doorway looking at Jarrod, who was still pacing the floor with an angry look on his face.

"I don't believe this shit," Jarrod said.

"Don't you have anything else to say to me?" Jackie asked.

The look Jarrod gave her sent chills down her spine, and she was once again afraid. She wondered if she should have waited until he was sober to confront him, but she knew she had to finish what she started.

"I guess it's safe to say this marriage is over," Jackie said, afraid to look at him.

Jarrod stopped in his tracks and said, "Excuse me?"

"I said, I think it's safe to say this marriage is over," she said louder.

Jackie felt the smack before she actually heard it. She stumbled backwards as she held the side of her face. Jarrod walked over to her and yanked off his belt.

"Bitch, this shit ain't over until I say it is!" He yelled, as he struck her repeatedly with the belt.

"Jarrod, please!" Jackie screamed, as she tried her best to shield her face from the force of his blows.

"Please what? You want it to be over bitch, *and* you fucking somebody else? I'll kill you first." Jarrod stopped hitting her long enough to catch his breath, and Jackie took that opportunity to scramble away from him and run to her now screaming baby.

Jarrod reached her just as she was about to enter the nursery and grabbed her hair.

"Where you think you going, bitch? I ain't finished with you yet."

With her last bit of strength, Jackie kneed Jarrod in the groin. He held onto her hair as he buckled in pain. Jackie clawed at Jarrod's hands and face and when his gripped finally loosened, she pulled away from him leaving behind a chunk of hair. Jackie shut and locked the door on Jarrod's hand as he reached for her once more.

With the baby now in her arms, Jackie picked up the extension and frantically called 911.

"Please help us!" she cried when the operator answered.

"Miss, please calm down, and tell me what's wrong," the operator said.

"My husband beat me up, and said he is going to kill me, please…"

"Okay, ma'am. What is your address?"

Jarrod began banging on the door and yelling obscenities as Jackie gave the operator their address.

"Please hurry! I have a newborn baby in here, and I think he may break down the door."

The banging abruptly stopped, and Jackie no longer heard Jarrod on the other side of the door.

"I have a two officers on the way to you. Now, I'm going to stay on the phone with you until they get there, okay?" The operator was trying her best to keep Jackie calm.

"Thank you," Jackie whimpered as she stepped closer to the door to hear what Jarrod was doing.

"Ma'am what is your name?" the operator asked.

"Jacqueline James."

"Is it okay if I call you Jacqueline?"

"Yes, please hurry."

"They are almost there. Jacqueline, what is your husband's name?"

"Jarrod." The operator relayed the information to the officers on the radio.

"Is there a gun in the home?"

"No." Once again the operator spoke to the officers.

Bam! Jackie screamed and jumped as Jarrod began pounding on the door.

"Jacqueline! Jacqueline! What's happening? What is he doing?"

"He's hitting the door with something." Jackie looked around the room for anything that could be used as a weapon. The best she could come up with was the lamp.

While Jarrod continued to try and beat the door down, the doorbell rang.

"I think they're here," Jackie whispered to the operator when Jarrod finally stopped banging on the door.

"What part of the house are you in?" the operator asked.

"We're upstairs. I'm in the baby's nursery but I don't know where he is. I don't think he's outside the door anymore."

Jackie crept to the door and listened. She heard the front door open and then Jarrod's voice as he spoke to the police.

"He's talking to the cops now," she said to the operator.

"Okay, Jacqueline. You're okay now. I'm going to let you go so you can speak with the officers, okay?"

"Thank you so much."

"If you need anything else, call us back. Good night."

Jackie put the phone down and went to pick up her crying baby. She opened the door and slowly walked to the steps. She heard Jarrod as he tried to convince the officers that nothing was wrong.

"My wife and I had an argument, that's all," Jarrod said

"Sir, that's not what your wife told the operator," she heard one of the officers say. When she reached the bottom of the stairs, she stayed there until she was able to regain her composure.

"You know how women can be. Sometimes they get emotional and overreact." Jarrod laughed, trying to lighten the mood.

"Sir, where is your wife?" one of the officers asked, getting impatient with Jarrod's small talk.

"She's upstairs putting the baby to sleep. But I'm telling you, everything is alright," Jarrod insisted.

"Sir, we need to speak with your wife. She is the person who made the call, so we need to hear it from her," she heard the other officer say.

"I'm right here," Jackie said as she entered the foyer.

Jarrod's face was fixed in a tight smile as her looked from Jackie to the officers. "Baby, can you tell the officers that everything is okay."

Jackie saw that Jarrod, ever the manipulator, must have cleaned himself up before answering the door. He bore no resemblance to the maniac who was beating her like a runaway slave only moments ago. She looked at the officers, both of whom were waiting for her response. Jackie read their badges from where she was standing. One of them, Officer Toth, a short and stocky white man, had his hand resting casually on his gun. And the other, Officer Knight, was a tall, dark and very handsome brother, who was staring at her intensely.

Jackie looked down at her baby in her arms and remained quiet. She knew she needed to say something, but she was embarrassed.

"Miss, is everything okay? You told the operator your husband threatened to kill you," Officer Toth said.

Out of the corner of her eye, Jackie saw Jarrod glaring at her. She shook her head as tears fell from her eyes.

"No, everything is not all right. He hit me, and he did say he was going to kill me."

"Jackie!" Jarrod yelled as he took a step toward her.

Jackie cowered and took a step back to avoid Jarrod's advance. Officer Knight put his arm out to block Jarrod from reaching Jackie.

"Sir, did you hit her?" he asked.

"No, I told you we had an argument and that's it."

The officer leaned in closer to Jarrod and pointed to his face. "Where did you get those scratches from, then?"

Jarrod's hand went to his face. The scratches on his cheek were now raised and beginning to scab.

"Oh these? Well, you know how it is when things get a little rough and tumble in the bedroom."

He chuckled to try and make light of the situation.

"You lying son-of-a-bitch. He did hit me," Jackie said, looking directly at Jarrod.

"Would you like to press charges?" Officer Knight asked.

Jackie shook her head. "No, I just want him to leave."

She hated the thought of going to court and having everyone know what happened. She would rather forget about it and move on with the rest of her life.

"Are you sure about that?" the officer asked. He could see the bruise on her face and the welts on her arms and couldn't believe she was going to let him get away with it.

Jackie took a deep breath and said, "Yes, I'm sure. I just want him to leave my home."

"Sir, we're going to have to ask you to leave." The officer was disappointed with Jackie. There was nothing he hated more than a man who hit women. He wanted so badly to take Jarrod into custody and work him over real good on the way to the police station.

"I'm not going any damn where! This is my house!" Jarrod yelled.

Jackie flinched and moved out of his reach.

"Sir," Officer Toth said firmly, "either leave, or we'll take you down to the station."

"I'm a lawyer! I know my rights!"

"Well, good for you. That means you can represent yourself," Officer Knight said sarcastically.

The rage was evident in Jarrod's eyes as he walked past Jackie to get his car keys. Officer Toth trailed Jarrod closely as he gathered an armful of his belongings and led him through the front door. After he left the house, Officer Knight handed Jackie a card.

"My name is Officer Knight. If he bothers you anymore, I want you to call me anytime, day or night."

"Thank you," Jackie said as she wiped her tears.

He turned to walk away, but spun back around before walking through the door.

"You know you really don't have to take that from him. You should really think about pressing charges, because if he did it once, he will do it again. Trust me, I see it every day, and sometimes it only ends with someone dying. Think about it," he said.

Jackie knew what he said was true, but she didn't want to think about it. "Good night and thanks again," she said to him while ushering him to the door.

Once she was alone, Jackie double-checked the locks and set the alarm system. First thing in the morning she was she going to get the locks changed and a new pass code for the alarm.

She was still afraid that Jarrod might return, so after she put Naomi in her crib, she locked the door to the nursery and slept in the chair with the phone in her lap.

DONNA

It was 4:00 when I packed up my things and left work. The law firm where I worked was typically busy on Mondays, so when my boss told me I could leave early, I left as quickly as I could before he changed his mind. I called Keith's office to see if I could persuade him to join me at home for an early dinner, but all I got was his voicemail. After the fifth call, I drove to his office.

Mrs. Knickson, the Office Manager, held the door for me as I entered the building.

"Hey, Donna-baby. You coming to see Keith?" she asked.

"Hi, Mrs. Knickson," I said as I gave her a hug. "Yeah, I got off a little early, so I figured I would come and get my man."

We both laughed.

"Good for you. I keep telling him he should slow down or else he's going to work himself to death."

"Tell me about it. Well, I don't want to hold you up, Mrs. Knickson. I see you are on your way out of here."

"It's okay. I ain't in any rush to get home," she laughed.

"It was good seeing you again, Mrs. Knickson, and tell your husband I said hello."

She frowned and said, "Good night, baby, and you take care."

I left her standing at the door while I waited for the elevator. When the elevator door opened, Mr. Reed stepped out.

"Hello, Donna," he said.

"Hi, Mr. Reed. I was coming to see Keith," I said as I tried to walk around him to the elevator.

Instead of moving, he looked over my head and said, "Nadine, I'll be right there."

I turned around to see Mrs. Knickson standing in the doorway with a strange look on her face.

"All right," she said slowly.

Mr. Reed was staring into my face when I turned around, so I took a step back.

"Excuse me," I said as I tried to move past him once more.

He licked his lips and let his tongue linger on his top lip longer than necessary. I felt ready to vomit as he let his eyes openly wander over my body.

"You know I've been meaning to talk to you, Donna."

"About what?" I sighed.

"How is everything going with you and Keith?"

"Everything is fine, thank you."

"Are you happy?" he asked, as he closed the gap I had created.

"Very. Why do you ask?" I was feeling very uncomfortable with his line of questioning, and the way he eyed my breasts made me feel dirty.

He fingered the necklace I was wearing and said, "My son has good taste."

"Mr. Reed, I really need to get going." I moved his hand away from my neck.

"I know about women like you…" he started.

"Excuse me? Women like me?" I put my hand on my hip and was about to read him the riot act before he interrupted.

"Not in the way you're thinking. I mean, I know what a beautiful woman like you wants and deserves. You know, the finer things in life."

"And your point is?"

"Do you think Keith can really provide you with the life you want? Can he be the man you need him to be?"

"Mr. Reed, are you serious? That is your son and my *fiancé* you are stabbing in the back. You are a piece of work." I shook my head in disgust. "Why would I want a man like you anyway? You are no good. At least I know Keith loves and respects me."

Mr. Reed spread his arms, "You know, you're right. Let's see, why would you want a man like me? Keith is a work in progress. I am what he is working day and night to become. I could give you everything your pretty little heart desires. Think about it." He had the nerve to wink at me.

"No, I'm thinking about going upstairs to tell your son what you are trying to pull. I can't believe you. I always knew your old ass wasn't shit. You are one fucked-up individual. And for the record, you need to be trying to be the man your son is."

I pushed past him and stepped in the elevator. Before the elevator closed, I nodded my head toward the door.

"By the way, Mrs. Knickson doesn't look too happy right now. You should probably get to her before she comes to her senses and goes home to her husband."

He turned around, and I pushed the button to close to door before he could say anything else.

I slumped against the wall of the elevator and took a deep breath. I had to laugh to keep from crying. My mother would probably slap me blind if she knew I passed up an opportunity to get with someone of Mr. Reed's status. My mother worked hard to raise her only daughter to be gold digger and for a long time, I practiced what she preached, until I met Keith. I can't lie, if Mr. Reed had made that same offer a few years ago, I would have dropped Keith like a bad habit. But I worked hard to give up my old ways, so I pushed Mr. Reed's proposition out of head and focused on my future with Keith.

When the elevator doors opened, I walked down the empty corridor to Keith's office. As I neared the end of the hallway, I slowed when I heard a man's raised voice coming from inside Keith's office. I heard Keith speaking in a quiet, even tone, apparently trying to calm the other person down, but the other person seemed to only get angrier. Even though the other person sounded familiar, I couldn't place the voice. Figuring it was a client, I turned around to wait in the front office. My heart stopped when I finally recognized who the man was on the other side of the door. I spun on my heels and nearly tripped over a trashcan trying to rush into the office. I stopped just outside the door and tried to regain my composure. It was all I could do not to burst into his office and kill them both. Instead, I decided to hear for myself what was going on instead of hearing Keith's explanation.

"Jarrod, you need to calm down," Keith said firmly.

"Don't tell me to calm down, you need to answer my damn question! What the hell did you and that bitch tell my damn wife?"

My breath caught in my throat when I heard him call me a bitch.

"I'm going to tell you one more time, calm down, Jarrod. Let that be the last name you call her." The tension in Keith's voice was evident.

"Fuck that! Jackie told me you and *your woman* talked to her, and now she's talking about a divorce!"

I silently pumped my fist in the air.

"Look, Jackie called the house one day, and she and Donna started talking, and…"

"And what? She started talking about shit that's none of her goddamn business? Tell me this, how did it get to the point when *you* talked to Jackie?"

"Look, I tried to stay out of it, but she kept calling me. What did you want me to do, lie?"

"You goddamn right I wanted you to lie. That was not your business to tell. Would it be cool if, say your father, asked me if you're gay, and I told him yeah, just because I don't want to lie?"

Keith sighed loudly. "Jarrod, you know that's not the same."

I had heard enough, so I opened the door and walked in. Keith noticed me first and his eyes nearly bugged out of his head. Jarrod on the other hand, looked like he could kill me. Based on their reactions, I would have thought they were guilty of something, if I hadn't heard what was going on with my own two ears.

"Hey, baby." Keith walked around his desk to greet me with a hug and kiss.

Jarrod rolled his eyes.

"What's going on in here, Keith?" I asked while looking Jarrod in the eyes.

"I want to know why you are minding my business," Jarrod said.

I pushed away from Keith and said, "Excuse me? You know, you got a lot of damn nerve. I told her because she had a right to know. I didn't find her, she found me. Blame yourself, because if you wasn't doing what you were doing, there wouldn't have been anything to tell!"

"Jarrod, I'm sorry about you and Jackie, but I couldn't lie to her, man." Keith said.

"What are you sorry for?" I interjected. "You need to be apologizing to me!"

"Donna…" Keith said.

Jarrod looked from me to Keith and shook his head. "You know what, Keith, fuck you and your apology! And fuck this little hoodrat too!" Jarrod pushed past us and stormed down the hall.

"I got your hoodrat, bitch!" I yelled to his back. I turned back to Keith. "I am so sick of him, and this whole love triangle

shit is getting real old, Keith. You know, if he was a woman causing all of this trouble, I would have beaten his ass already."

Keith ignored my comment as he sat down and put his
head into his hands. "This is exactly what I didn't want to happen,
Donna."

"What are you talking about?" I asked as I crossed my
arms.

"I told you I didn't want to be involved in this mess with
Jarrod and Jackie."

"And I told you, you're already involved. You are just as
guilty as Jarrod."

"I don't want to talk about this anymore. Let's just forget
it. What brings you down here today?"

"Don't change the subject, Keith."

"Donna, give me a break. I've had a long day and I'm
tired."

"You aren't the only one who's tired, Keith. How many
times am I supposed to go through this with you and him and act
like it's normal?"

Keith gathered his briefcase and keys without saying a
word.

"Keith?"

"Donna, what do you want from me? I did everything you
asked me to do. You act like I asked him to come here. I mean,
what did you expect, for me to confess to his wife that I had an
affair with her husband and there would be no repercussions? Did
you really think he would go away quietly after that?" He walked
past me and out his office without another word.

I walked up behind him as he waited for the elevator and said, "What I expect is for you to be a man and tell him to stay away from us. Look at me, Keith." I tugged at his sleeve. "Put yourself in my shoes. How much of this would you be willing to take?"

He held the elevator for me to enter and nodded his head. "I hear you," he said.

*   *   *

The following weekend I went to the mall to pick up some things for Jackie's little girl. After the run-in with Jarrod, I spoke to her and she confirmed that she had indeed confronted him and asked him for a divorce. We made plans to go to lunch, but at the last minute, Jackie cancelled because her mother-in-law didn't feel well and couldn't watch the baby. Jarrod was no longer living there, so I told her I would come to her house and visit since I hadn't seen the baby yet. I invited Keith to come along, but he refused, saying he didn't feel comfortable facing Jackie just yet. I didn't push the issue, so I left him in the house and headed to the mall to buy a gift for the baby.

Keith and I did not speak about Jarrod after we left his office, but there was still tension in the air. Feeling that I may have pushed him too far, I got out of the doghouse by selling the majority of his remaining tickets to the AIDS Awareness Fundraiser to some of my co-workers.

On my way to Jackie's house, I took a detour and stopped by my mother's house. I hadn't talked to her since the argument on my birthday weekend, and I wanted to see how she was making out.

My mother lived not too far from my old apartment. When my grandmother passed away, my mother moved out of the projects where she raised me and my brothers and moved back into my grandmother's home. My grandmother would turn in her grave if she saw how run-down her beloved house now looked. There were beer bottles on the front steps and an old loveseat on the porch that, I assumed, was being used to replace the stolen porch furniture. I saw no signs of life in the small garden. The roses, orchids, and lilies that my grandmother tended to with as much love and care as she cared for us died with her. I took a deep breath before unlocking the door and walked into the stuffy house. The house was dark except for a light coming from the kitchen and a little sunlight seeping through the dusty curtains.

"Mom," I called out as I walked toward the kitchen.

"Donna? What you doing here?" Kevin, my younger brother, answered.

The smell of marijuana assaulted my nostrils when I reached the kitchen. Kevin was sitting at the kitchen table puffing on a blunt and putting powdered cocaine into little bags.

"What the hell are you doing, and where is Mommy?"

"Man, look, don't come in here with that shit. I'm doing what I gotta do to make some things happen."

"Make what happen? The police running in here and locking both you and Mommy up? I thought you were looking for a job."

"I got a job, and it probably pays more than yours. Shit, I

got my own business, and I make my own hours," he said with the blunt hanging from the corner of his mouth.

"Being a block hugger and selling packs for Snoop is not having your own business. You are going to wind up in jail just like Marvin, or worse, dead like most of the guys you grew up with. You know better than I do that this drug game isn't like it was before when it was enough to go around for everybody. These dudes are hungry and will take your shit."

Marvin, my oldest brother, was arrested when the mayor initiated a citywide task force to rid the streets of drugs and guns. He was caught when the police raided the stash house he was in. Marvin was convicted and was now awaiting his sentence.

"I ain't going nowhere, and I damn sure ain't worried about nobody taking my shit." He reached under the table and pulled out a gun.

I took a step back. "What the fuck are you doing with that, Kevin?"

"What you think I'm doing with? I'm protecting my shit, as you call it." He put the gun back under the table and resumed bagging the cocaine and puffing his blunt.

"And how you just gonna be in here smoking a blunt? You know better than to be that disrespectful."

"Oh, here we go. Don't act like you don't blaze."

"If I do, it's in *my* house, and I damn sure never did it in Mommy's house where she can walk in on me."

"Whatever, Donna. I do what the fuck I want around here. I'm the man of the house, and I take care of Mommy, not you.

She knows what it is, so mind your business. She told me how you wouldn't help her out with the bills and how you acting all stuck-up since you been with that corny-ass Keith."

"Whatever, Kevin. I shouldn't have to take care of Mommy. Not as long as you're here. When I give her money, she just spends it on you, and I'm not taking care of you too. Like you said, you're the man of the house, so you give her money for the bills."

"I got this. You just better hope that dude don't leave yo' ass and you have to come crawling back here." He laughed at his comment as though it was the funniest thing in the world.

"Don't worry about me. I'm good. Where is Mommy at, anyway?" I was tired of the conversation, because I could see I wasn't getting anywhere with him.

"She went to the market. Ms. Neesy let her use her Access Card to get some food."

"Ms. Neesy's still doing that, huh. Damn, I thought they gave out the Access Card to stop people from selling food stamps. Well, tell Mommy I came by to see her."

I leaned in and gave Kevin a kiss on the cheek. Despite the fact he was a pain in the ass, I still loved my little brother, drugs and all. He finally put that blunt down and stood up to give me a tight hug.

"It was good seeing you, even though you get on my nerves," he laughed. "Let me know if that dude fucks up, and I'll whip that ass."

I laughed. "I know, Kevin, and thank you, but, trust me, he ain't lettin' this go," I said while twirling around. "Damn, and speaking of that, I gotta give y'all my new number. I moved in with Keith a couple weeks ago."

I reached into my purse and pulled out a pen and paper.

"Moved in with him? That's what's up. Now we can have a bangin' ass cookout in your yard."

"Not hardly. You and Mommy are welcome, but none of your trifling ass friends." I gave him the paper with my number written on it. "Don't forget to give this to Mommy. I gotta go."

"Okay," he said after sitting back down.

"See you later, and please be careful."

"Don't worry about me, Sis, I'll be okay. Trust."

I left my mother's house, happy that she hadn't come home. I did not want to have to deal with both her and Kevin's nonsense.

I arrived at Jackie's house an hour later carrying the bags of baby clothes and toys I purchased from the mall. When she answered the door, we hugged and I followed her to the kitchen. I sat the bags down and looked around. Her kitchen was magnificent, with hardwood floors and cabinets, granite counter tops, and stainless steel appliances. I immediately fell in love with the refrigerator, which was huge and designed to look like one of the cabinets. The kitchen alone was almost the size of the apartment I had in South Philly.

"You look good, Jackie," I said while she finished preparing the baby's bottle. It was impossible to tell she had just had a baby a few weeks ago. She wore a pair of fitted jeans and a tank top that revealed a flat stomach. I hoped I would look that good after I had children.

"Thank you, girl," she sighed.

"Where is the baby?"

"She's in the living room taking a nap." She looked at the clock on the stove. "She'll be waking up any moment now, and I know she's going to be hungry."

"So, how has everything been?" she asked as I followed her to the living room.

"You know how it is, same stuff, different day."

Naomi, who was a spitting image of Jackie, was asleep in her swing. I smiled at Jackie and said, "She is absolutely beautiful, and look how long her eyelashes are. She almost makes me want to have one."

Jackie sat down next to me on the couch, and I was able to get a closer look at her face. She looked like she had been crying. Her eyes were pink, and there were dried tear streaks on her face.

"Are you okay, Jackie?" I asked her.

"I'm okay. Why do you ask?"

"Because it looks like you've been crying."

She swiped her hand across her face and sighed. "It's just been hard since Jarrod left. He's being even more of an ass now that he's gone."

I nodded my head, but remained silent.

"Do you know I had to call the cops on him to get him to leave?"

"You're kidding."

She nodded. "Promise me you won't tell anyone, Donna. Not even Keith, okay?"

"I promise. What is it, Jackie. Did he hurt you?"

She held her head down and nodded. "He started accusing me of having an affair with another man because I didn't want to have sex with him."

"Talk about having a lot of nerve."

"I know, and after I told him that I knew about him being with Keith, I told him the marriage is over and he freaked out on me. He hit me." She tried to blink away the tears.

"Oh Jackie, I am so sorry. It's a good thing you called the cops. There is no telling what he might have done. So, are you going to press charges?"

"No, believe it or not, I still love him, and I don't want my husband and the father of my child in jail."

I stared at her silently. I couldn't believe she said that.

"I know you think I'm crazy. It's okay. You're not the only one. When my mother-in-law found out, she went ballistic. She told me I was a fool if I let him get away with it."

"You told her about Keith too?" I asked.

She shook her head, "No, I couldn't do that. I just told her I found out about another woman, which is not exactly a lie."

I sighed deeply. "Well, the most important thing is that he's gone," I said, trying to reassure her.

The baby stirred in her swing, and Jackie picked her up.

"You want to feed her?" she asked me.

"Yes, but let me wash my hands first." She pointed me in the direction of the bathroom.

After leaving the bathroom, I looked at the family photos she had prominently displayed on the walls. As I looked at her wedding photo, I wondered what went wrong, because in the picture Jarrod looked at her as though she was the only woman in the world. I could only hope Keith would not change the way Jarrod did after our own wedding.

I made it back to the living room just in time to see the baby open her eyes. Jackie gave me the baby blanket and placed Naomi in my arms.

I fed and burped the baby while Jackie and I continued our conversation.

"So how have you been, otherwise?" I asked.

Jackie stood up and walked to the window. "I feel like a fool for even caring about him. Do you know he emptied our joint bank account? I went to the bank to withdraw some money, and they told me the balance is $1.67. I thought they made a mistake, so I had them check and then double-check it, but it wasn't a mistake." She turned around to face me. "There was over $60,000 in that account. I don't understand it. He is the one who cheated on me with a man and is cheating with God only knows who else, and he acts like I did something wrong. I mean, I have a baby I have to support."

I was in shock. Jarrod had turned out to be more of an asshole than I thought.

"Jackie, you can't be serious. He actually left you with nothing?"

She nodded her head slowly.

"Well, do you have another personal account you can draw from, at least until you can do something about him taking the other money?"

"I have an account that I used for direct deposit when I was working, but there's only about $750 in there."

"Can I help you with anything? I'm sure Keith would help out in any way he can."

"Donna, you are the only person I've told about this. I don't want anyone else to know, and I certainly don't want people to start feeling sorry for me."

"Have you talked to him?"

Jackie walked back over to the couch and sat down. "After I came from the bank, I left messages on his cell and his office, but he wouldn't answer. I thought he would be at his mother's house, but she hasn't seen or heard from him."

I had heard from Leah, Sabrina's younger sister, that Jarrod had been staying at Sabrina's place, but I didn't want to tell Jackie that.

"So he never called you back?" I asked.

"Yeah, a few days later. I asked him why he would take all of our money, and he said it was his money and, since I had the house, we were even. He told me that he wouldn't support a house he didn't live in."

"That is horrible. What about his mother, can't she do something?"

Jackie rolled her eyes at my question. "He can't stand his mother, and he won't take her calls at all. She offered to give me some money to help out, but this is not her problem. To tell you the truth, I don't know what to do, Naomi is too young for me to go back to work, and I couldn't bear putting her in daycare." She started to cry. "My mortgage is due in two weeks, and I have no idea how I'm going to pay it. The worst part of it all is he doesn't even care about what happens to his baby."

I put Naomi back in her swing and hugged Jackie. "Why don't you call my boss? He's a really good lawyer. Maybe he can do something about getting you some support from Jarrod."

Jackie turned away from me to blow her nose.

"I spoke to Mrs. James about it, and she said the same thing. She's a lawyer too, and she was talking about getting some kind of emergency order of temporary support, but I don't know if I can even wait that long."

She stopped talking and nervously rubbed her hands on her pants.

"So what are you going to do?"

She was about to answer and then stopped. I searched her face for an answer, but she averted her eyes away from my stare. A thought entered my mind and I hesitated to ask, because I was scared of the answer.

"Jackie?"

"Hmm?" She would not look at me.

"Please don't tell me you're thinking about letting him back in here."

"If I do, it would only be until I am able to get myself on my feet."

"You can't be serious, Jackie. I can't believe you are even considering letting that Ike Turner wannabe back in the house. What if he does it again?"

"I don't know, Donna. I haven't made a decision yet. Like I said, if I do it, it'll only be until I can go to work and be able to support me and Naomi. I don't plan on living like husband and wife. I will probably move into the guest room next to the nursery."

"It sounds like you have really thought about it and already made up your mind."

The telephone rang before Jackie could respond. Naomi, who was startled out of her slumber by the incessant ringing, began to wail. While Jackie went to take the call in the kitchen, I tried to rock her crying baby back to sleep. Although I wasn't trying to eavesdrop, I overheard part of Jackie's conversation. She was telling the person pretty much the same thing she told me, and, from what I could tell, the person on the other end of the phone was not happy with her logic.

I heard her explaining something about mortgage payments and then refusing help from anyone. After several minutes, she told them she had company and she would call them back.

Jackie came back into the living room and took Naomi out of my arms. She looked at her baby for a long moment and kissed her tenderly on the lips before laying her on her chest.

"If you were in my shoes, what would you do? With no money, a baby to support, and a bunch of debt?" Jackie asked me.

"Truthfully, I would have had him arrested and taken his ass for everything he's got. You know it's not too late to press charges."

"I know. The person I was just talking to," she said, motioning toward the phone, "his name is Sean, and he's one of the cops who came here that night."

I raised my eyebrows in a question.

"I was thinking about getting a restraining order in case Jarrod tried to come back and hurt me, so I called the officer to find out what to do. And we've talked on and off ever since. He's been trying to talk me into pressing charges, but I don't really want to do that. When he called a few minutes ago, I told him that I was thinking about letting Jarrod back in, and his reaction was pretty much the same as yours."

"Sounds like he might be trying to do more than just his civic duty. It sounds like he likes you," I said.

Jackie shook her head, then stopped and smiled. "You think so?"

"How naive can you be? Come on, girl. Why do you think he's still calling you? Get real."

I couldn't believe this was the same woman who cussed me out something terrible, not even three months ago. It's no wonder Jarrod played her like her did. She was too gullible.

"I don't know. I thought maybe he cared or something."

"And why would he care unless he likes you? I wouldn't be surprised if he asks you out before this is all over with."

Jackie turned her head so I wouldn't see her blushing.

"He already did, didn't he?" I asked.

"He said he didn't think I should sit in the house and mope, so he invited me and the baby to lunch."

"Damn, you move fast, don't you? Did you go?" I laughed.

"No, I didn't feel right. Only a couple of people know that Jarrod isn't here, and the last thing I need is for somebody to see me out with another man."

"Girl, look, you have to stop worrying about what other people think. It's time to worry about you. Jarrod is the one who fucked up, not you. He ought to be glad you haven't posted flyers telling everybody he's a wife-beating freak."

Jackie stayed quiet for a moment then asked, "Is that what you did to Keith?"

I didn't know if I should take offense to her question or not. I looked at her face to see if she was intentionally trying to throw what Keith did in my face.

"No, but Keith didn't hit me either, and since then he's been faithful." I smiled, trying to convince both her and myself at the same time.

"I guess I have a lot to think about."

"When will you know for sure?" I asked.

She shrugged her shoulders

I looked around for the gifts I bought for the baby. "Let me show you what I bought for Naomi. I think you'll like it."

I reached for the bags and put them down next to her.

"Oh yeah, I almost forgot I about that. Can you hold her while I open them?"

I took the baby from her and watched while she emptied the bags.

Before I knew it, three hours had passed. Once we stopped talking about her issues with Jarrod, the conversation was much better. I didn't want to overstay my welcome, so I told Jackie I would call her the next day. Jackie walked me to the door, and we hugged goodbye.

"Call me if you need anything, okay?" I said as I walked to my car.

"Thanks for coming by, Donna. I really needed that," she said as she waved goodbye.

As I drove away, I had a sick feeling that the next time I talked to Jackie, she would tell me that Jarrod was back home.

KEITH

"Donna, come on! I don't want to be late!" I stood at the foot of the stairs, impatiently waiting for Donna to drag herself from in front of the mirror.

"I'm coming, I'm coming! Goodness gracious, you act like it'll be the end of the world if we're ten minutes late," she said as she finally came down stairs.

I had to say it was worth the wait. Donna was definitely going to be the finest woman in the building. I silently breathed a sigh of relief when I saw what she chose to wear. Earlier in the day, she came home with a garment bag and refused to let me see the dress, saying she wanted it to be a surprise. I was nervous, because I was expecting to see something very short and very tight. So it was a pleasant surprise to see her in an emerald green, floor-length gown that was very conservative.

"How do I look?" she asked as she twirled around.

I laughed out loud when I saw the back of the dress, which had a deep plunge and came to the very top of her butt. She just couldn't resist showing some skin.

"You look beautiful," I said as I helped her with her shawl. "One thing, though."

"What's that?" she asked as she patted her dress.

"Promise me you won't bend over," I teased.

"Stop playing, Keith, I thought something was wrong," she said as she playfully pinched my arm.

Even with me rushing Donna, we were still late due to traffic and trying to find a parking space. The fundraiser was being held at the First District Plaza in West Philly, and because there was another event being held there, all of the prime parking spaces were taken. When we finally arrived, we were met at the door by Pastor Douglas and his wife, Ms. Elaine, who were taking the tickets. I peeked my head into the room and was pleased to see a full house.

"I see we have a good turnout," I said to Pastor Douglas.

"We sure do," he said as he waved to a few of the other arriving guests.

Donna was in deep conversation with Ms. Elaine and did not see me signal her to go inside.

"Hello, ladies. I hate to break this up, but, Donna, I think we should go in and find our table before it gets too crowded."

"All right baby, I'll talk to you later, Ms. Elaine," Donna said as I ushered her into the ballroom.

Our table was situated in the far right corner of the room, and already every seat was taken. My father was seated next to a woman who I assumed was his date by the way she was clinging to him. I read the place settings just to be sure we weren't at the wrong table.

"I think those are our seats," I said politely to the couple occupying our seats.

"Oh, I'm sorry," the man said as he turned around to face me.

"Keith," my father said as he stood up. "You remember Corey, don't you?"

My mouth went dry as I tried to compose myself. I reached out to shake Corey's hand.

"Of course I remember Corey. How have you been?"

He shook my hand and held my gaze. I broke his stare before someone, like Donna, caught on to the chemistry between us.

"I've been good, thanks. How about yourself?"

"I can't complain." I wiped my sweaty palm on my pants and averted my attention to Donna. "This is my fiancé, Donna. Donna, this is Corey, I took over his post in the league when he moved to D.C."

"Nice to meet you. This is a good friend of mine, Mia." He gestured to the pretty woman standing at his side.

She smiled at me, and I shook her hand in greeting.

"So, what brings you back in town?" I asked.

"It was kind of spur-of-the-moment. I spoke to Ronald a couple of days ago and he mentioned this fundraiser, and the rest is history. I didn't see my name on any of the placeholders, and when I saw your father sitting over here, he invited us to sit with him. I hope you don't mind."

"No, it's no problem at all. It's good to see you," I said.

My father stepped in between Donna and me. "Corey

was just telling me that he's thinking about starting up a chapter of the Black Men's Empowerment League down in D.C. I told him he should recruit a few of the members here to help get it up and running. You should think about it, Keith. I can handle anything that comes up at the office."

Donna nudged me before I could respond. "Baby, I'm starving. I'm going to go and get us some plates before these hungry Negroes eat it all." She turned to Mia, "You want to come with me? They could be here all night talking about this stuff."

Grateful for the interruption, I offered to go instead. "I'll go with you, baby. I want to see what all they have over there."

"Keith, please, like I don't know what you like to eat." She winked at me. "You coming, Mia?"

Mia looked relieved that Donna had asked and jumped at attention. "I am right behind you."

"Make sure you bring me back some potato salad," I called to Donna.

I watched them walk away and tried to think of a way to tell Corey that I couldn't come. I knew my father would not understand my refusal to help Corey after all he'd done for me. For years growing up, all I'd heard my father talk about was the league this and the league that, so much that I didn't want to go anywhere near it when he tried to bring me on as a junior member. It was Corey who got me to come to my first meeting and eventually join the league.

"Keith. Keith?" My father's voice brought me out of my haze. I turned around and was met by Corey's gaze.

"I'm sorry. What's up?" I asked.

"What do you say to helping Corey?" My father's frustration with my hesitation was evident.

"Let me see what I can do," I said, looking at Corey, "I'll let you know for sure some time this week. Give me your number, and I'll call you."

"I have something even better than that. I planned on staying in town a few more days to catch up with some family and friends, so maybe we can do lunch later in the week. That way we can go over the details and I can try and convince you to give me a firm commitment…to the project." I hoped I was the only one who caught the innuendo in his statement.

"Now, that sounds like a plan," my father said as he patted both of us on the back.

I scanned the room for Donna, who seemed to taking an obscene amount of time to come back with the food. She and Mia were just reaching the end of the buffet line with their arms full of food. I took that opportunity to get away from Corey and my father.

"Let me go and see if she needs help carrying those plates." I nodded my head at the other two couples sitting at our table. "Plus, we are going to need to find some other seats," I said.

"I'll walk with you. I can't let you show me up in front of my woman. I'll never hear the end of it," Corey said, refusing to let me off the hook.

"Don't worry about the seats. I'll take care of that. You go on ahead and get your food," my father said. As we walked over to the buffet table, I overheard my father sweet-talking one of the other couples into moving elsewhere.

"So how have you been otherwise?" Corey asked me as he struggled to keep up with my fast pace. "Congratulations on your engagement. She's very pretty."

"Thank you. She's a very special woman," I said. The DJ came in over the music to welcome everyone and let us know that the chairman of the league would be addressing the crowd in the next ten minutes.

"You know, it really is good to see you, Keith. From what I hear, you've filled my shoes quite well."

"Now, look what the devil dragged in," said a voice coming from over my shoulder.

Corey and I turned around to see Jarrod standing there with a smirk on his face and a drink in his hand.

"Hey, Jarrod, good to see you, man," Corey said as he and Jarrod shook hands.

Jarrod looked from me to Corey and nodded his head. "So what's going on? You two catching up on old times, or what?"

I ignored his question. "How long have you been here? I didn't see you earlier."

"Were you looking for me?"

Corey, who looked uncomfortable with Jarrod's behavior, tugged my arm. "Jarrod, we were on our way over to help our ladies with the plates, so we'll have to continue this later."

Jarrod shot Corey an angry look, "Yeah, whatever."

We got away from Jarrod as quickly as possible. "Thanks, man," I said.

"No problem. He hasn't changed has he?"

"Nope. Once a jackass, always a jackass."

Donna and Mia waved us over and handed us the plates. "I was wondering how long it would take you to get over here and help us," Mia said.

"Can you take these over to the table, baby? I have to use the ladies room," Donna said before she and Mia hurried off to find a restroom.

As promised, my father had two empty seats waiting for us when we returned. I picked at my food and remained quiet as my father and Corey discussed some of the issues going on within the league.

The music quieted down and the emcee came on the mic asking everyone to take their seats. I stood up and pulled out the chair next to mine when I saw Donna approaching the table.

Donna looked at the chair and said, "Switch seats."

"Huh? Why?" I asked.

Donna looked at my father, who had stopped his conversation to watch us. She lowered her voice and leaned close to me, "Can we please switch seats? I would like to sit next to Mia."

For the sake of keeping the peace, I did as she asked. "I don't see what the big deal is," I mumbled under my breath.

We ate our food while we listened to Ronald, the chairman of the league, and Pastor Douglas tell us how the money donated so far would be spent. By the time the speech was over, everyone in attendance was willing to give their entire life savings to the pastor. When the DJ started playing some old-school music, Donna asked if I wanted to dance. It was either fall asleep from all of the food I ate, or dance to work it off, so I chose to work it off. We danced for three songs straight, until the DJ mixed in some line dancing music.

"You want some dessert, baby?" Donna asked.

"You can bring me some carrot cake if they have it," I said, pleased that Donna seemed more attentive to me and my needs for a change. I knew I shouldn't get used to it, but I figured I would enjoy it while it lasted.

I was enjoying the sight of the couples bopping on the dance floor, but my mood quickly turned sour when I saw Jarrod staggering in my direction. I knew if Donna came back to see him at our table, my whole night would be ruined, so I stood up to leave.

"I'll be back," I said over my shoulder.

Jarrod reached the table before I could get away. "Whoa, brotha, where you off to?" he asked, sitting next to my father, who was in deep conversation with his date.

"I'm going to find Donna."

He laughed loudly, and everyone at the table turned to look at him. "There you go again, chasing after that woman. Man, you must really be sprung. I ain't seen you act like this about *anybody* in a while." He turned and looked directly at Corey. "You know what I'm saying, Corey."

"Yeah well, I guess I am. After all, she is my woman." I started to have a bad feeling about Jarrod and his reason for coming to my table.

"Your *woman* huh?" he slurred.

At that moment, I decided to call it a night. "I think I'm

going to get out of here. Dad, can you give Corey my number?"

"What's the rush, Keith?" My father asked.

"Yeah, Keith, what's the rush? Why don't you stay tell us all the story of how you met Corey." He gestured to everyone at the table. "This is a good one y'all, so listen up. Come on, Keith, tell it."

"Jarrod, what in the hell are you talking about? We already know how they met." My father said.

Donna walked to my side and tapped my arm. "What's going on, Keith?"

"Nothing, baby. I was just coming to find you. Are you ready?"

"What's wrong, Keith? Why don't you want to tell the story?" Jarrod asked.

Corey stood up and asked, "Jarrod, what is it that you want?"

Jarrod ignored Corey and turned to my father. "Mr. Reed, I don't think you know the whole story. You see, Keith and Corey were…"

Corey grabbed Jarrod by his collar and said, "Shut up."

"Jarrod," I said, "I think you've had too much to drink."

Jarrod pulled away from Corey and yelled, "Get the hell off of me!"

The music lowered as everyone else in the room turned to look at us.

"Jarrod, you're drunk and I think you need to leave," my father said.

Pastor Douglas walked over and stepped in between Corey and Jarrod. "What's going on over here? What's all the commotion about?"

"Hey, Pastor Douglas," Jarrod said a little too loud. "I think you would like to hear this too. I was just about to tell the story of how Keith and Corey became such good friends." He turned to face the crowd of on-lookers. "As a matter of fact, I think all of you would enjoy this story!"

"Keith, what is this fool talking about?" Donna asked as she pulled my arm.

"Nothing, let's get out of here."

We turned to walk away when Jarrod yelled, "What is it, Keith? Are you afraid of what people might think if they knew you and your predecessor were fucking?"

There was a collective gasp throughout the room, and my heart stopped cold. I spun around to shut Jarrod up once and for all, but Corey got to him first. He was able to hit him about four times before the pastor was able to pull Jarrod out of his reach.

Corey turned to Mia and said, "We need to leave."

She backed away from him and shook her head. "What is he talking about, Corey?"

My father looked at me with a grimace and asked, "What in the hell is he talking about, Keith?"

"Nothing, he's drunk." I turned to the crowd, who stared back at me in surprise. "Somebody get him out of here!"

No one moved. I looked into the faces of the member's of the league, but they all averted their eyes and ignored my silent plea for help.

Jarrod struggled to his feet and looked out into the crowd of shocked spectators.

"Does anyone want to get me out of here? 'Cause I'm sure a few of you have some skeletons." Groans could be heard throughout the crowd as wives looked at their husbands in question. "Is anybody really going to step in and try to shut me up?" No a word from anyone. "I didn't think so."

His attention returned to me. "Are you going to deny it, Keith? Tell them how you and Corey slept together up until he moved to D.C."

It was my turn to attack Jarrod. I punched him in the mouth and sent him flying over the chair.

I looked at my father, whose face was in a scowl. "Dad…"

He cut me off. "I have nothing to say to you."

I grabbed Donna's arm and pushed my way through the crowd, and we didn't speak until we were in the car.

"Keith, please tell me he was lying," she cried.

"I wish I could," I said as I sped through a red light.

She put her head in her hands. "Oh my God. I can't believe this. Did you cheat on me with him too?"

"I'm sorry, Donna. No, it was before I met you." I shook my head to trying to erase the memory of what Jarrod had done.

"So you really slept with that man?" She looked at me incredulously.

"Donna, I told you I had been with one other man besides Jarrod."

"When did it happen? How did it happen?" she asked.

"It's not important. It happened a long time ago."

"Tell me, Keith!"

"Let it go, Donna, I don't want to talk about it." I gripped the steering wheel and tried to focus on the road.

"Keith, you owe me that much, I want to know."

"I said, let it go," I growled.

I tuned Donna out as she continued to ramble on, and thought back to the night that started it all.

After my first encounter with Jarrod, in college, I made sure to avoid him as much as possible. I no longer studied in our room, opting for the library instead. I made sure to return to the room only to sleep. That worked well until I came down with a bad cold, and my trips to the library were cut out completely. Jarrod helped me out by getting my assignments and fixing me canned chicken soup.

When I felt better, Jarrod invited me to a party off-campus. He told me the party would be like something I had never seen. I was cool with going, because neither he nor I had made any mention of that night since it happened.

Excited about the prospect of meeting some women, I jogged to my car and told Jarrod I would follow him. But he insisted we ride in his two-year-old Nissan Maxima, a gift from his parents for finally being accepted into a decent college.

"You ready for this, man?" Jarrod asked.

"Yeah, I mean, it's just a party, right?" I asked.

"Yup, just a party."

We pulled into the parking garage of what looked like an old warehouse. "What is this, a rave?" I laughed.

"Nah, but I promise you'll like it," he said.

When got into a big freight elevator and rode to the top in silence. I was about to ask exactly who was giving this party when the elevator signaled our arrival. We walked down a bare and dimly lit corridor until we reached the only door without a padlock. Jarrod used a funny-looking key to open the door, and we entered a hot room that was eerily quiet for a party.

"Yo, man, what type of shit is this, and where in the hell did you get that key?"

"Relax, the key is our invitation to the party. You can't get in unless you have one. Now, stop bitchin' and follow me."

We walked a few paces until we came to another door. Jarrod knocked four times in rapid succession, and the door opened. This room was completely different. While it was as dim as the first room, this room was full of people: men in business suits, some in jeans, and some wearing baseball caps and Timberlands. The music was tight, and the drinks were flowing. I was so happy we weren't at another "dollar" party that it took me a few moments to realize I didn't see any women. I turned to Jarrod, but he'd already left me to go to the bar. I tried to catch up with him, but stopped in my tracks when I saw him tonguing our English Lit professor.

When I reached him, I tugged his arm and asked, "What the fuck is going on here?"

He snatched his arm back and sneered, "Man, don't

front like you ain't down with this shit. Grow the fuck up!"

I couldn't believe it. "Jarrod, I'm leaving. This shit ain't cool, man. What if somebody sees us?"

"And what? What are they going to do, tell? Look around you, man These brothers don't give a fuck about you and your reputation. They have more to lose than the both of us put together. Well, Professor Taylor might tell Dean Adams."

I could have killed him because the sick bastard was laughing.

"I'm fucking with you! Look." He pointed, "Dean Adams is right over there."

"Holy shit," I muttered.

"Yeah, 'holy shit' is right. Now, take my advice, enjoy yourself. The free parties don't happen as much as they used to. Most of the parties are charging for membership now. I'll catch up to you later, say 1:00? We can meet by the door."

"Yeah, I guess I don't have a choice. You're driving."

"I know." He winked at me and returned to the professor.

I went to the end of the bar and ordered a Long Island Iced Tea. While I sipped my drink, I looked around and couldn't help thinking how out of the loop I was. I was in awe that there was a whole underground world that I knew nothing about. These were professional men, street thugs, and everyday brothers you would never suspect. The homo thugs were who surprised me the most, because I knew these were the same brothers who would be the first to gay bash. Most of the men had wedding rings prominently displayed on their left hands. I looked over my shoulder and saw the dean and about three men disappear into a back room. There were several other doors lined up along the same wall. I ordered another drink and downed it. According to my watch, it was 11:00 and I had two hours to kill, so I decided to take a tour of the place.

A short and stocky brother blocked my path and held out his hand.

"How you feelin', man? What's your name?"

I shook his hand and immediately snatched it away when I felt his index finger stroking the palm of my hand.

He looked offended, but pressed on. "Can I buy you a drink?"

"No thanks, I'm good."

The man stepped closer to me and I got a better look at is face. He looked about sixty years old and had a bad case of acne. He also sported a receding hairline with a greasy ponytail.

"So are you going to tell me your name, or what?" He was sweating profusely and seemed to be getting impatient.

"Oh, my name is Jack," I lied.

"Hi Jack. My name is Cecil. You want to…"

"Cecil, I was just on my way to the bathroom, and I'm leaving after that, so I don't really have time to talk. It was nice meeting you, though." I cut him off before he could *make his proposition. This man was old enough to be my father and was in no way enticing.*

"But I just saw you come in."

I stepped around him and walked away as quickly as I could. I made my way over to the wall of doors. I tapped lightly on the door I saw the dean enter, but got no answer. I cracked the door and saw Dean Adams on his back, legs in the air with one man pounding his ass and another feeding him his dick. I shut the door before anyone noticed me and leaned against the wall. After I caught my breath, I knocked on the door farthest from the crowd.

"Yeah?" a voice from the other side of the door called out.

I opened the door and saw a man sitting on one of the two couches in the room.

"Come in. I just needed to get out of there for a minute," he said.

"It's okay. I was just checking the place out. I'll let you get back to, um whatever it is you were doing."

"Oh, I see," he laughed. "You must be new to this. You look a little intimidated. That's it, huh? It's all over your face. Well, you can come in. I promise I won't bite." He put his hands up in a sign of peace.

I walked in and pushed the door closed. The room was barely lit, so it took my eyes a second to adjust to the light. I sat on the couch closest to the door and took in my surroundings. The room looked as though it belonged in a brothel. Very tacky. The walls were covered in what looked like black velvet. The couches were butter-soft gray leather, and the rugs were zebra print fur. I noticed next to the couch I was sitting on was a table that held a bowl full of condoms.

"So, do you like what you've seen so far, ah, what's your name?" he asked.

"Oh, it's Keith."

"Good to meet you, Keith, I'm Corey. So, do you like what you've seen so far?" he asked again.

"What?"

"I mean out there. Is it what you expected?"

"To tell you the truth, I was expecting a regular college party. My roommate brought me here."

"Really? Well, how could he be so sure you wouldn't mind coming to an event like this?"

I lowered my eyes to the floor.

"Oh, I see. Well, no need to worry, your secret is safe in here."

"Yeah, he told me that." I had to strain my eyes to see my watch. 11:15pm

"You know, these parties take place about once a month at different locations. If you become a member, you get the perks, one of which is exclusive invitations to our VIP parties."

"What's a VIP party?"

"Just what it sounds like. You can meet some of your favorite entertainers and athletes, as well as make some life-long networking connections. I assume you're a student, so

I'm sure the networking opportunities would be especially beneficial to you."

"Are you a member?"

"Better than that, I founded it." He smiled. "So who's your roommate? Is he a member?"

"His name is Jarrod, and, no, he's not a member, at least, I don't think so."

He frowned. "Yeah, I know Jarrod." He paused for a minute and then continued, "I don't know how close the two of you are, but watch yourself around him."

I opened my mouth to speak, but he held up his hand.

"Hear me out, He seems to be a manipulative young man, a little angry even. I've come across people like him, and it rarely turns out good. So just be aware."

He got up from his couch. "I'm going to get a drink, can I get you anything?"

"No, I'm good, thanks."

When he left the room, I sat back and exhaled loudly.

I could kill Jarrod for doing this to me, *I thought.*

I looked at the table with the condoms and shook my head. Then someone tapped on the door. I reached over to open it and Corey walked in holding two drinks. He pushed the door closed with his foot and sat down next to me.

"Here you go. I figured you could use one of these," he offered.

"Um, thanks. What is it?"

"It's Hennessy and Coke. They're pretty good."

I took the drink and swallowed half. Now that he was

on my couch, I got a good look at his face. He sort of favored the guy from Groove Theory, the guy all of the women swooned over, Bryce something. He didn't strike me as someone who would be into this stuff, but hell, the same could be said for me. I looked at my watch again, 11:40.

"You have somewhere to be? You keep checking your watch."

"Nah, but I'm supposed to meet Jarrod at 1:00." I downed the rest of my drink.

"Feel free to stay here. I'll keep you company."

"Thanks." I leaned my head back and rested my head on the overstuffed pillows.

I felt Corey moving closer, and then he leaned over me. I tried to sit up, but his chest was pressing into my face.

"What are you doing?" I asked.

He continued reaching and said, "I'm just locking the door."

"For what?"

"I don't want to be disturbed. I came in here to catch a breather."

I started to get up. "Well, I'll leave you alone then. Nice meeting you, and thanks for the drink."

"No." He put his hand on my leg. "You're okay."

I sat back down. My heart was pounding, and the drink started to take its desired effect.

"Relax," he said.

His hand remained on my leg. He gave it a little squeeze, and when I didn't object, he began massaging my thigh. I started getting aroused, and it was evident by the bulge in my slacks. He continued massaging my thigh and then moved up to my zipper. I looked at him, unsure of what to do. Before I knew it he had my dick out and in his mouth. I closed my eyes and thought about making him stop, but I couldn't. He licked and sucked until I was ready to cum. Then, just as suddenly as he started, he stopped.

"You liked that, didn't you?" he asked as he tried to kiss me. I turned my head, and he kissed my cheek. Kissing another man was out of the question.

"No kiss? That's cool. There's something else I would rather do, anyway." He took his pants off and began stroking his own erection. "Take your pants off. I want to feel you."

My eyes nearly popped out of my head. Did he want to fuck me? Up until that point, I only had the one experience with Jarrod.

"Nah, man. I can't get down with that." My dick went totally limp.

"No? A virgin, huh? Well, I'm not, so come on."

He got down on all fours with his ass in the air. When he saw I didn't move, he turned around and saw my dick hanging limp. He grabbed it and started sucking again. When he was satisfied that I was hard enough, he got back on all fours. I took my pants off, took a condom from the bowl, tore it open, and put it on. I moved over to Corey and knelt down.

"Don't worry, you can't hurt me. Put it in."

I pressed the head to his ass, and he moaned. I pushed a little harder, and it went in easier than I had expected. I began pumping in and out, softly at first, but Corey had other ideas.

"Come on, fuck me," he grunted as he started thrusting against me.

He groaned loudly and laid down flat on his stomach. The movement caused his ass to contract against my dick, and I ground harder into his ass.

"Oh shit!" I hissed as I came. I sat up, exhilarated. That was like nothing I had ever experienced. Corey turned over and smiled at me while he stroked himself. It was a few seconds until he came, but when he did, he let out a guttural moan. I got up, took the rubber off, and tossed it in the trash. I picked my pants up from the floor and put them on. All the while Corey lay in a semi-conscious sleep. I sat on the couch and thought about what happened.

Does this mean I'm gay? Maybe not, because I still love women, *I thought.*

I was more confused than ever. I looked at my watch, 12:30. Time to get moving. I walked over to Corey and said, "Yo, I'm out."

He flagged me away, and I turned and left.

When I returned to the party, it was beginning to wind down, and there were a lot fewer people than before. Maybe the wives started calling. I didn't see Jarrod, so I sat at the bar. I ordered a double shot of vodka.

"Thanks," I said when the bartender sat it in front of me. He nodded and walked away. I was sipping on the drink when I saw Jarrod coming from the other side of the room.

He was followed by Professor Taylor and two men who looked like gang members. I started making my way over to where he was when Corey stepped in front of me.

"I wanted to catch you before you left. I hope you enjoyed yourself." He handed me a business card. "Take this and call me. No strings attached. Our committee has a lot of opportunities for bright young brothers like you. We've got to look out for each other." He patted me on the back and walked away.

The card read:

Corey Harper

CFO- Black Men's Empowerment League

PO Box 26152

Phila., PA 19106

I knew all about the league. My father had been a member for years and was very involved.

I caught up with Jarrod at the door as he was saying his goodbyes to the professor and his new friends.

"You ready?" I asked.

"Yeah."

The professor looked in my direction, and I averted my eyes. As we walked to the elevator, I saw Corey, and he nodded in my direction.

Jarrod noticed and said, "What's up with that?"

"With what?"

"Dude over there, I saw you up in his face earlier and now he's over there staring you down."

"I wasn't in his face. He invited us down to that Black Men's Empowerment League my father belongs to."

"Yeah whatever. I know what I know. And you smell like ass." He walked ahead of me. "Man look, I ain't dumb okay? Don't think I didn't see you and dude coming from the same room." Jarrod looked as though he wanted to fight.

I swallowed deeply and thought long and hard before answering. "Oh yeah, after you ran off with your boys, I went looking for someplace to hide. I met Corey in one of the empty rooms and we just kicked it for the rest of the night. It was nothing. As a matter of fact, what the fuck do you care? I ain't questioning about who or what you were doing." I feigned anger to get Jarrod to back off of trying to find out the details of my evening.

"Like I said, I know what I know."

When we got in the car, Jarrod continued to try to pry information about Corey from me, but I denied everything. He gave up when he saw I wasn't budging and started telling me how Professor Taylor liked to be fucked. I tuned him out and thought about my own evening. As much as I didn't want to admit it, I did enjoy Corey's company.

Over the next few years, Corey and I worked closely on the league's various committees and remained friends. Occasionally, we would indulge in sex, with Corey on the receiving end. That continued until Corey got engaged to a senator's daughter and moved to D.C. But before he left, he appointed me his successor as chief financial officer.

I pulled in front of the house and turned the car off. Donna, who was now quiet but still very angry, took her seatbelt off and opened the door. I reached over her and pulled the door closed.

"Wait," I said.

She turned to me with tears in her eyes and said in an angry voice, "Wait for what, Keith?"

"Let me explain."

She sat back in her seat and closed her eyes. "I'm listening."

"Look, I met Corey back when I was in college, and, yes, we messed around for a few years. But that was before I met you."

"Okay, and what else?"

"There used to be parties held all over the city that only a few select people knew about, and I met Corey at one of those parties."

I sighed loudly and continued to tell Donna a condensed version of the way I met Corey. When I was done, I could not look her in the face, because I was too embarrassed

"You mean to tell me that there are parties where a bunch of undercover brothas get together and fuck?"

"Yeah, I guess you could put it like that. But I want you to understand something, Donna. When Jarrod invited me, I had no idea it was that type of party. I didn't know until I got there. Hell, I never even knew those things even happened."

"So when was the last time you've been to one of those *parties?*"

I shook my head vigorously. "That was the first and the last one."

We were quiet for a moment, and then she looked at me as though a thought just occurred to her, "So who else knows about these parties?"

I chuckled, "That's the funny part. A few of the league members are involved, which is why no one wanted to step up to help tonight. Half of them were probably disgusted, and the other half were scared shitless. Donna, you would be surprised at who goes to these things. I mean, athletes, judges, politicians…the list goes on. These are people who are married with children, and there wasn't a lot of safe sex going on either."

"What about your father?" she asked, sitting up in her seat.

I laughed out loud. "Are you kidding me? He's probably the straightest man I know." My laughter turned to groans. "I don't know how I'm going to look my father in the face after this, or anyone else, for that matter."

"Think about how I feel. I'll forever be known as the woman with the gay husband." She looked at me apologetically. "Sorry, you know what I meant."

"I wouldn't blame you if you decided to leave, Donna. I really wouldn't."

The thought of her leaving my killed me inside, but I really couldn't expect her to stay with a black could hanging over her head.

"I'm not leaving you, Keith. Shit, after what you told me about these parties, why would I go and find someone else, only to find out they're on the down-low? I might as well stick it out with you. At least I know the deal."

I couldn't believe she said that. "I guess that's a good way to look at it."

"Now, if you cheat on me, I'm going to have to fuck you up. Don't get it twisted. I love you, but I ain't stupid."

I tapped my fingers on the steering wheel. "I guess I'm going to have to face my father pretty soon, but I think I'm going to work from home for a few days."

"Damn, I hope this doesn't get out," she said.

"It may, but you might be surprised. Trust me, most of those people in there really don't have room to throw stones. The only person I'm worried about is my father and how he's going to react when I see him."

Donna looked at me and said, "Keith, there is something I think you should know. I should have told you before but I didn't want to rock the boat."

"What?" I hoped she wasn't going to tell me she'd slept with someone else. I didn't think I could take any more drama in one night.

"Your father has been coming on to me lately. It started that night we saw him at the Four Seasons and a couple of times after that."

My throat went dry. "Why didn't you tell me this before?"

"I don't know. The last time he did it, I told him I was going to tell you, but that was the day I came to your office and Jarrod was there."

"What did he do? Did he touch you?"

"No, he basically told me I should leave you and get with him. I'm telling you now, because I don't want you to feel bad about having to face him, because what he's trying to do is much worse than what he can say to you."

I slammed my hand on the dashboard. "Mother-fucker!" My night was getting worse by the minute.

Donna flinched and said, "Keith, I'm sorry I didn't tell you before."

"No, it's not you. Come on, let's go in."

We didn't say much to each other until we were settled in bed. I thought back to all of the times my father has tried to undermine me or put me down, and all of those old feelings resurfaced.

"I wonder if the pastor will talk about homosexuals in his sermon again on Sunday," Donna said.

I chuckled.

"Imagine that," I said under my breath.

"Did you see the look on his face after Jarrod said that about you and Corey?"

She laid her head on my chest, and I ran my fingers through her hair. "Yeah I saw the look on his face." I paused. "As far as his sermon is concerned, if he knows like I know, he better not say too much. How does the saying go, 'thou dost protest too much'? Now is not the time for him to draw too much attention to himself."

Donna shot up like a bolt of lightning. "What are you trying to say, Keith? That the pastor is gay?"

"I wouldn't call him gay, but he certainly likes his men. He and Jarrod have been getting down for a while now."

"Shut up!" She slapped her forehead. "This shit is getting ridiculous. Are there any straight men left in the world? Poor Ms. Elaine, do you think she knows?"

I shrugged my shoulders. "I don't know and don't really care. I have my own problems. Besides, she has my father to comfort her if something happens."

Donna slowly shook her head and laid back down. "I'm going to sleep. I don't want to hear anymore."

I kissed her forehead and closed my eyes, praying that I would wake up and find this entire night had been a bad dream.

JACKIE
AND
JARROD

Jarrod left Sabrina's house, promising to return the next day after work. He surprised himself by keeping her around, although she was no longer of any use to him. He couldn't help it. Sex with her was almost as good as it was with men. She also never pressed him to use condoms, which made it so much more fun for him. Sabrina opened her home and her bed to him when Jackie had him removed from their home and took pleasure in playing house with him. Jarrod liked the attention he received from Sabrina, because it reminded him of early in his marriage, when Jackie couldn't get enough of trying to please him. Although he loved the attention Sabrina gave him, he knew he could never make a life with her. She was not good enough, which was why he convinced Jackie to let him move back home on a trial basis. He knew that emptying the bank account was a low blow, but he also knew that a lack of money would virtually cripple Jackie.

Oh yeah, he thought. *She liked to talk that independent shit, but when it came down to it, she is nothing without me. Did she really think she could make it without me? And now that there's a baby involved, it makes it that much harder for her to leave me.*

It took Jarrod about two weeks to finally get back home, and it wasn't easy. When he arrived to the house, Jackie told him the ground rules. He could keep the master bedroom and she would take the guest room. That suited him just fine. He didn't find her as attractive since she'd had the baby anyway. Next, she told him she would not cook, clean, or do laundry for him. That also worked for him, because he had Sabrina to do those things. It was Jackie's last statement that nearly threw Jarrod into another rage. She said that she had no intentions on staying with a man who disrespected her by cheating and hitting her. Her plan was to go back to work as soon as Naomi was old enough and save enough money so that she could support herself, and then begin the divorce proceedings. The only thing she wanted from Jarrod was child support for Naomi and nothing else. Jarrod played along, but inside he seethed. He thought her whole plan was bullshit. He imagined Jackie taking him to court and getting half of his hard-earned money in a divorce settlement. Jarrod had other plans. The only way he planned to let Jackie out of the marriage was in a casket. He had no plans of paying for her or her baby.

"The only divorce she'll get is an OJ divorce," he said to himself.

Jarrod drove to the gym prior to going home to work off some pent-up stress. After what happened at the AIDS fundraiser, Jarrod had received several calls from other members of the league warning him to keep his mouth shut. He assured them that they had nothing to worry about, and that his problem was with Keith, not them. Moments after Keith left the fundraiser, Corey left, but not before telling Jarrod to watch his back. The room started buzzing as soon as Corey was out of earshot, causing Mr. Reed, Keith's father, to make a fast exit. Jarrod stumbled around the room, telling anyone who was willing to listen the story of Keith and Corey's secret relationship. Pastor Douglas attempted to calm Jarrod down, but thought better of it when he remembered Jarrod's threat to reveal more secrets. Instead, he stepped up to the podium and thanked everyone for coming out, then told them to take as much food as they wanted and to drive safely.

As he remembered the panic-stricken looks on the men's faces, Jarrod laughed out loud. He knew that after what he'd done he would no longer be welcome at the league. But he wasn't worried. He'd accomplished what he set out to do. Jarrod was no longer focused on getting Keith. It was more like getting back at Keith for telling Jackie, and, in his eyes, it couldn't have turned out more perfectly.

When he arrived home, Jarrod heard Jackie on the tele-phone in the bedroom. He wanted to pick up the extension in the kitchen to see who she was talking to, but decided against it. Instead, he checked the answering machine while he looked through the mail. He deleted the message from his mother telling him to call her. The next message was from his doctor's office telling him they'd been trying to reach him and them asking him to call in as soon possible. Jarrod looked at his watch and decided to call them in the morning. He'd gone in for a physical the week before and they told him everything looked good, so he wondered why they were calling him now.

Jackie entered the kitchen, interrupting his thoughts.

"Your mother asked for you to call her," she said.

"What did she want?"

Jackie shrugged her shoulders. "I didn't ask."

Jarrod walked into the living room to watch television while Jackie went to tend to the baby. They spent the rest of the night without seeing each other.

*   *   *

The next day after Jarrod left for work, Jackie went to the post office to apply for a post office box and to then to the bank to open an account that Jarrod would know nothing about. After running a few errands, Jackie returned home to find Ms. James waiting for her in the driveway.

"There's my precious grandbaby," Ms. James said as she took Naomi from her car seat. "Hey, Jackie. I figured I would come over and have lunch with you since I was in the area."

Jackie unlocked the front door and carried the bags into the house. "Oh, I'm sorry. I wish I had known, I could have prepared something for you."

"No, it's my fault. I should have called first, but it was a spur-of-the-moment decision," Ms. James said.

"I can make us some sandwiches, if you like," Jackie offered.

"Don't worry about it. I can pick something up on the way back to the office. Sit down and relax."

"It's no trouble, I need to eat something anyway. I think I'm losing too much weight too fast."

"You know what that is, don't you?" Ms. James said as she cuddled Naomi. "It's stress."

Jackie remained silent while she made the sandwiches. Oddly enough, Jackie truly liked Ms. James, but sometimes she could be a little overbearing. Most times, Jackie appreciated Ms. James' blunt advice, but this was one time she didn't feel like hearing it. Jackie placed the sandwiches, chips, and drinks on a tray and carried it into the living room, followed closely by Ms. James and Naomi. They ate quietly, both deep in thought about Jarrod. Jackie was planning how she would be able to handle being a single mother, and Ms. James thinking of how wrong her son was. Ms. James was the first to break the silence.

"Did you hear about all of that commotion Jarrod caused at the AIDS fundraiser last weekend?"

Jackie shook her head. "No. I know he went, but we didn't talk about it or anything. What happened?"

"Well, apparently, Keith, your friend from college, was sleeping with one of the men who used to be on the committee, and Jarrod got drunk and outed the both of them."

Jackie coughed as she tried to dislodge the food caught her throat. "What?"

"Yes, and now it is all over town. They said Keith's father is too embarrassed to even show his face. Can you believe that? I tell you, you young people are into things that were just not acceptable in my day. I don't know what the world is coming to."

No longer hungry, Jackie put down her sandwich. "How did you find out?"

"I heard about it in the hairdresser. I'm telling you, by now everyone has heard about it."

"Why would Jarrod do something like that?" Jackie mumbled to herself.

"Are you really surprised, Jackie? He's been doing a lot of crazy things lately, wouldn't you agree? Look what he did to you. And while we're on the subject, I, for the life of me can't understand why you would let him back into your home after he put his hands on you."

This was exactly the conversation Jackie wanted to avoid, so she didn't say anything.

"Jarrod's father tried to put his hands on me once," Ms. James continued, "and trust me, by the time I was finished with his ass, he knew not to ever try it again."

"What did you do?" Jackie asked, unable to resist.

"I cut his ass! He got so scared, he ran right out of that house in his underwear."

Both of them doubled over in laughter. "Ms. James, you are crazy."

Ms. James turned serious. "No Jackie, Jarrod is the crazy one. What if he does it again?"

"I don't think it will happen again." But even as she said it, Jackie didn't feel so sure.

"Jackie, look at me." Jackie looked up, "He has already shown you who he is, so why won't you believe him?"

Jackie shook her head in confusion. "What do you mean?"

"I mean, Jarrod had already shown you his true nature, so you need to trust that he will reveal himself again. A leopard doesn't change its spots."

The telephone rang, and, grateful for the interruption, Jackie jumped to answer it.

"Hello?"

"Hello, may I speak with Jarrod James?" the woman on the phone asked.

"He's not in. May I ask who's calling?"

"This is Dr. Robinson's office calling. Could you ask Mr. James to give the office a call as soon as possible?"

A little alarm went off in Jackie's head. She knew they called yesterday, but she thought nothing of it at the time. But now that they were calling back again, Jackie became frightened.

"May I ask what the problem is?"

"I'm sorry, ma'am, but we need to speak with Mr. James."

"Well, I'm his wife and if something is wrong, I need to know."

Ms. James, alarmed by the urgency in Jackie's voice, came to see what was wrong.

"What's wrong?" she mouthed.

Jackie held up a finger to silence her and continued her conversation.

"You're his wife?" the woman asked.

"Yes, now, what's wrong? Is Jarrod sick?"

"Mrs. James, I'm going to need to ask you to come down

to Dr. Robinson's, the sooner the better. And, if possible, bring Mr. James in with you."

"Can't you tell me what's going on?'" Fearing the worst, Jackie was getting sick to her stomach.

"I'm sorry, but I am not at liberty to discuss it over the phone. You will have to wait until you see the doctor. How soon do you think you can be here?"

"What time do you close today?" Jackie asked frantically.

"We're here until six, but we take our last appointment at 5:30."

"We'll be there." Jackie hung up the phone. She had to squeeze her hands together to keep them from shaking.

"What's going on? Is something wrong with Jarrod?" Ms. James asked.

"I don't know. That was his doctor's office. They want us both down there today."

Jackie picked the phone up and dialed Jarrod at the office, but got no answer. She tried his cell phone, but it went straight to voicemail.

Jackie grabbed her keys and turned to Ms. James. "Can you stay here with Naomi for a little while? I need to go and find out what's going on."

"Of course. I'll call the office and tell them I won't be back."

"Thank you, and if Jarrod calls, tell him to meet me at Dr. Robinson's office," Jackie said as she opened the door.

"Call me as soon as you can."

Jackie didn't hear Ms. James' last statement. She was already halfway down the driveway.

Ms. James closed the door and sighed loudly. She planned to try and talk Jackie into leaving Jarrod once and for all and starting a new life. Ms. James was not one of those mothers who defended her son when he did wrong. In fact, she knew that she was a better mother because she recognized his faults and held him accountable. Jackie had become the daughter she'd always wished for, and that meant she wanted the best for her. Naomi cooed from her swing.

Ms. James picked her up and said, "Don't worry little one, your Mom-Mom is going to help your mommy come to her senses and get you guys out of this mess your daddy created. Oh, who am I kidding, Naomi? You can convince a fool against her will, and she will be a fool still. Let's just hope she sees just how wrong this whole marriage is."

After speaking with her secretary, Ms. James carried Naomi to kitchen to prepare her bottle and waited patiently for Jackie's return.

*   *   *

Thirty minutes later, Jackie was sitting in the waiting room of Dr. Robinson's office. When the nurse called her name, she stumbled over a nearby chair in her rush to get into the doctor's private office. Dr. Robinson, who was seated behind his desk, rose to greet her when she entered the office.

"Hello, Mrs. James," he said while taking her hand.

Jackie studied his face for a sign of what he was going to say next. "Hi. I got down here as soon as I could."

"Is Mr. James coming?"

"I left a message for him to meet me here, but I don't know if he's coming."

He looked disappointed. "Well, I must say, I hoped to speak with the both of you together."

"Doctor, forgive me if I'm being short, but if there is something wrong with my husband, you need to tell me."

"Of course." Dr. Robinson looked down at Jarrod's chart. "Mrs. James, has your husband talked to you about any problems he's experienced recently?"

Jackie shook her head. "No. What kind of problems?"

"A few weeks ago, Jarrod came in for a routine physical, and during my examination he complained of frequent diarrhea and headaches. As a precautionary measure, we ran a battery of tests, one of which was what is called an enzyme immune assay, which is used to detect the HIV infection." Dr. Robinson paused to allow his words to sink in. "Unfortunately, Jarrod tested positive for HIV."

Jackie was not sure she heard the doctor correctly. She thought he said Jarrod was HIV positive, but that wasn't possible. Jarrod certainly didn't look sick, so surely the doctor was mistaken.

"Mrs. James?" Jackie looked at the doctor with a confused look on her face. "The reason I asked you to come down is because I think it's best that you get tested for the virus as soon as possible. It is imperative that we know your status so, if necessary, we can treat it accordingly."

The reality of what Dr. Robinson said hit Jackie like a kick in the gut. She bolted out of her seat and crumbled to the floor. After hearing the wails coming from the office, the nurse rushed in to help Jackie up and back into her chair. Dr. Robinson kneeled down in front of her and handed her a tissue. He and the nurse stayed by her side as she sobbed and babbled incoherently. The nurse's heart broke for Jackie as she saw another tragedy unfold right before her eyes, and she tried her best to console her.

Several minutes later, Jackie was finally able to speak. "Are you sure? I mean, what if the test is wrong?"

Dr. Robinson shook his head. "After his initial test came back positive, we retested the same blood sample to get a confirmation. I promise you, I wouldn't tell you this unless I were absolutely sure."

"So you think I have AIDS too?" Jackie hated the sound of her words and covered her face with her hands.

"No, Mrs. James. Not AIDS, HIV. And if treated promptly, many people can live with the virus for years. That is why I suggest you get tested as soon as possible. I would ask that you do it today."

Jackie remained quiet as she digested the information. She silently wept while thinking of how her life was now ruined. It killed her to know that her baby might have to grow up without her.

"OH MY GOD! My baby! What about my baby?" she screamed. She stood up and paced frantically around the office.

"I just had a baby. Does that mean that my baby could be infected?"

Dr. Robinson sighed. "Well, I can't say for sure. It depends on if you are infected and also when the virus was contracted." He paused. "I hate to ask you this, Mrs. James, but do you know how your husband could have contracted this disease? Is there any intravenous drug use? Or have there been any extramarital affairs?"

Jackie slowed her pace and said through her tears. "No, he doesn't use drugs, but he has slept around on me." She slumped into a chair. "God, how could I have been so stupid?"

"We are going to try to get in touch with your husband to discuss treatment options, but in the meantime, we are going to need to know the names and contact information for any people either of you have had sexual contact with."

"I haven't slept with anyone but that bastard," she said after blowing her nose. "And he, on the other hand, has slept with half the town. Men and women." The doctor raised his eyebrows. "Oh, I guess he didn't tell you that, Doctor. You see, my husband is an undercover faggot, which is probably how he got this shit. And now, I might have it. I know one thing, if there is anything wrong with my daughter, so help me God, you won't have to worry about treating him for shit, because I'll kill him myself." Jackie grabbed her purse and opened the door.

"Mrs. James?" Dr. Robinson walked around his desk, "Can I ask you to come back here with your baby first thing in the morning to be tested?"

"We'll be here." With that, she slammed the door and ran to her car.

Inside her car, Jackie pounded on the steering wheel and screamed out loud. She hated Jarrod for ruining her life and possibly Naomi's life. Her hands shook so badly that it took six tries before she was finally able to dial Jarrod's cell. She threw the phone on the floor of the car when his voicemail picked up, then slowly drove home.

When she pulled into the driveway, Ms. James opened the front door to wait for her. Seeing that Jackie remained in the car, she walked over and tapped on the window.

"Jackie?" She called through the window. "Why are you crying? Open the door!" Ms. James pulled on the door handle. Jackie wept openly and unlocked the car door.

"What's going on, Jackie?" she asked after helping Jackie into the house.

As Jackie told the story of what the doctor had to say, Ms. James listened intently. She hugged Jackie and assured her that everything would be okay. On their knees, they held hands and prayed for God to have mercy and spare the lives of Jackie and Naomi. Ms. James spent the rest of the night consoling Jackie and waiting patiently for Jarrod's arrival home.

Jackie woke up on the couch the next morning to find that Jarrod had not returned home. Ms. James left a note saying that she would return that afternoon and to call her if she needed anything.

Jackie tossed the note on the floor. "What I need is for this nightmare to end," she said to herself.

After checking on Naomi, who was sleeping soundly in her bassinet, she called Jarrod and left an urgent message on his cell phone telling him to call her. An hour later, Jarrod still hadn't called her, so she packed Naomi's bag and headed to Dr. Robinson's office.

When she arrived at the reception desk, she was ushered into an examination room, where she waited several minutes for a nurse to arrive. Jackie watched solemnly as the nurse swabbed the inside of Naomi's mouth. Tears ran down her cheeks as she opened her own mouth and allowed the nurse to do the same to her. Dr. Robinson entered the office and explained to her what would happen after the test was completed. He thanked her for coming in and told her he would have the results in two-to-three days.

"Today is Thursday, and with the lab being closed on the weekend, you can have your results on Tuesday at the latest. I will, however, try to expedite the test, but I can't make any promises.

I will call you personally as soon as I have the results. Good luck, Mrs. James," he said as he shook her hand.

Neither Jarrod nor Ms. James had returned when Jackie arrived home. She called Ms. James and told her not to worry and that she was going to try to get some rest while Naomi napped.

"Are you sure you'll be okay? I was on my way back over there anyway," Ms. James said.

"I'm sure. I'll call you later."

"Have you talked to that son of mine? I called him all morning long, but he's not picking up."

"No, not yet."

"This is exactly what got his ass in this situation now. Out there with God knows what woman and bringing diseases home to his wife and baby."

"Ms. James, I don't think Jarrod got it from a woman."

"What are you saying?"

"I'm saying that Jarrod is bisexual. That was the reason I left him in the first place." Even through her pain, Jackie felt relieved to have gotten that off of her chest. She now realized that the more she kept Jarrod's secret, the more she stayed in denial. She no longer felt the need to protect him, because he damn sure wasn't worried about protecting her.

"*Bisexual?*" Ms. James screamed.

"Yes. I found out that not only does he cheat with women, he also like men."

"Shit, that ain't bisexual. His ass is gay. If a man fucks another man, he's gay, not to mention, greedy! Why didn't you tell me before, and why on earth would you let him back into your home?"

Jackie didn't have an answer. With her mortality staring her in the face, Jackie couldn't give one good reason why she had allowed him to come back. All of a sudden, the money, the bills and her marriage were not worth her vitality. She just prayed that the tests would come back negative.

"Listen to me," Ms. James continued. "When he comes

home, you put his ass right back out on the street. Send him back to the trash that he got it from."

"That's if he comes home. He won't answer my calls."

"Oh, he'll come home. Criminals always return to the scene of the crime."

"Okay, Ms. James. But that was already the plan anyway. I'm done. I don't want him in my life or Naomi's. He's done nothing but cause me pain and hurt. Naomi is the only thing he's done right."

"I don't believe this," Ms. James said. "This explains all of his insecure, woman-hating ways." She sighed deeply. "Call me as soon as he comes home, Jackie, and if he lays a hand on you, you better try your best to knock his goddamn head off."

While Jackie appreciated Ms. James advice on how to handle Jarrod, she knew that "knocking his head off" would be no small feat, so she came up with another plan instead. After ending her conversation with Ms. James, Jackie went upstairs and began packing all of Jarrod's belongings. Several hours later, Jackie dragged the trash bags full of clothes and shoes down the stairs and placed them by the front door. While waiting for Jarrod to return home, Jackie bathed Naomi and put her to bed. The minute she heard Jarrod's car in the driveway, she ran into her bedroom and made a phone call.

Jarrod pulled into the driveway at 11:35. He debated leaving again when he saw all of the lights on in the house. The last thing he needed was to hear Jackie's mouth asking him a bunch of questions. After spending last night with Sabrina and all day with Pastor Douglas, he was dead tired and not in the mood for anything but sleep. But, somehow, he knew that would be asking too much. Both Jackie and his mother called him a total of twenty-seven times since yesterday, not including the messages left with his secretary. He didn't understand why they were bothering him, because he was only doing what Jackie asked. She told him she didn't want to live as husband and wife, so he was going to continue to live like a bachelor until she came to her senses. He'd even contemplated bringing Sabrina to the house, just to prove to Jackie that she could be easily replaced if he chose to do it.

"What the fuck is going on?" Jarrod said, nearly toppling over the trash bags partially blocking the front door. He looked up in time to see Jackie coming down the stairs with fire in her eyes.

"What the hell is all of this, and why do you have it blocking the door? I almost broke my neck," he said.

"I wouldn't be that lucky," Jackie said as she stood in front of him.

"What? You know what, I'm not dealing with your fat, miserable ass tonight." He tried to step around her, but she blocked his path. "Move!" he yelled.

"Dr. Robinson called yesterday."

"And?"

"And apparently you tested positive for HIV, you fucking faggot! And there's a chance that me and my baby might have it!" She picked up the bag that contained his shoes and pushed it into his chest, causing him to fall backwards. "I fucking hate you, you bastard! Get out!"

"Bitch, get the fuck out of here talking that mess," he said as he struggled to get up.

"Get out!" Jackie screamed at the top of her lungs. "You dirty freak, I hate you!"

Before Jackie could say another word, Jarrod charged into her, causing both of them to tumble to the floor. Jackie rolled away from him, but in one swift move, Jarrod flipped her over and put his hands around her neck. She struggled to breathe as Jarrod attempted to squeeze the life out of her.

"Bitch, didn't I tell you I would kill you?" Jackie felt herself weakening and prayed that Jarrod's face would not be the last thing she saw before dying. "You trying to tell me about some AIDS shit? I knew you was fucking somebody. Now die, whore!" Jackie tried to fight Jarrod off, but it was no use. He was too strong for her.

The front door was kicked open, and three uniformed police officers barreled in, tackled Jarrod to the floor, and handcuffed him.

One of the officers rushed to Jackie and called out to her, "Jackie? Are you okay? I got here as soon as I could."

Her eyes were open, but bloodshot, so to be on the safe side, he called for an ambulance.

Still sore from Jarrod's grip, Jackie slowly nodded her head. "Thank you for coming."

Had it not been for her quick thinking, Jackie could have been dead. Earlier, when she heard Jarrod's car in the driveway, she called Sean and told him she was afraid for her life. And, after seeing how close she'd come to dying, Jackie said a silent prayer of thanks for Sean's coming to her rescue.

Sean took her hand and helped her to a chair. He took one look at the bruises beginning to form on her neck and walked over to Jarrod, who was lying face down on the floor.

"Get up," he said.

Jarrod, who was handcuffed, looked up and said, "Fuck you. How the hell am I supposed to get up?"

Jarrod's ribs cracked from the impact of Sean's boot. "Now you're resisting arrest," he said.

Jackie winced at the sight of Jarrod being tossed around like a rag doll, but it felt good to see him in pain for once.

Jarrod howled when Sean snatched him to his feet. "Now, you little bitch, you like to hit women? Fight a man."

Even in pain, Jarrod couldn't resist having the last word. "I know my rights. I am going to sue you and the whole damned police force."

Sean slammed Jarrod into the wall and whispered in his ear, "Keep talking shit, and I'll make sure you don't make it to the police station. Now, make a move, and I will beat the dog shit out of you."

Jarrod looked at the other two officers for help, but they turned their heads and took Jackie's statement.

The EMTs gave Jackie the once-over and left just as quickly as they came.

"So I take it you're pressing charges, right?" Sean asked lightly.

Jackie smiled and hugged him tight. "Thank you so much,

he almost killed me," she cried as she buried her head into his chest.

"Hey." He lifted her head up. "That's what friends are for, right?"

She nodded.

"All right, let's get him out of here," Sean called to the other officers.

Jarrod, who had slumped to the floor in pain, yelped as the officer yanked him to his feet and pushed him out the door.

Jackie hugged Sean once more before closing the door behind him, then cried herself to sleep.

First thing in the morning, Jackie put Jarrod's clothes on the curb for trash pick-up and called a locksmith. She called Ms. James and retold the story of the previous night's events, and the two women shared a bittersweet laugh at Jarrod's expense. After getting the baby dressed and fed, she went down to the bank to make a withdrawal. Jackie walked out of the bank $54,000 dollars richer, headed over to her new bank, and made the hefty deposit. With a new-found confidence and respect for herself, Jackie was ready to face whatever came her way. Now all she had to do was wait for the test results.

DONNA

"Stop, Keith!" I screamed while trying to wrestle him off of me. "You win!"

"Why should I stop? You started it," he said while tickling me. I was laughing so hard, tears were running down my face and soaking the pillowcase.

It started the night before, when I jumped on top of him while he was sleeping and began poking him in the ribs, trying to wake him. He grunted and pushed me off of him after vowing to return the favor.

In the middle of dreaming about our upcoming wedding, I was awakened by Keith snatching off my comforter and tickling my feet.

"I'm sorry!" I yelled, squirming in the middle of the bed.

"Say, 'uncle,'" he laughed.

"Uncle!" When he stopped, I playfully nudged him onto the floor. I lay there breathing heavy and laughing at the same time.

"I told you, payback is a bitch," he said from the floor.

"Shut up," I said, throwing a pillow at him. He jumped up

and dove on top of me with his fingers in position to tickle me again.

"Okay, okay, I'm sorry. Please, don't do it," I begged.

Keith looked ready to go in for the kill, but instead he kissed me deeply. "This is what I love most about you," he said softly in my ear. "You are just as silly as I am."

I laughed and rolled on top of him. He smiled at me and reached up to pinch my nipple.

"Ouch," I yelled as he pushed me off of him and ran into the bathroom.

"I'm going to get you!" I called after him.

"I'm the king of the world!" he yelled from the bathroom.

I looked at the clock and saw that I had slept longer than I had planned to. It was already 10:30 and I had a hair appointment with Sheena at 11:00. While waiting for Keith to get out of the bathroom, I called the salon to try a get a later appointment.

I spent fifteen minutes on the phone with Sheena, pleading with her to squeeze me in, but she was booked solid until Tuesday. Looking at myself in the mirror confirmed that there was no way I could make it until Tuesday. So, I did what I vowed I would never again do, I swallowed my pride and called Sabrina's salon. I dialed the number and prayed she wouldn't be the one who answered.

"Thank you for calling In The Cut. This is Jasmine. How may I help you?"

"Hey Jazzy, it's Donna. Does Lena or Nita have any openings this afternoon?" I blurted my question out before I lost nerve.

"Hey, Donna." She lowered her voice, which let me know

Sabrina was within earshot. "Umm, let me check the book." I heard her shuffling pages. "Yeah, Lena is free until 3:30, so you can come anytime until then."

"That's good. I'll be there at one. Tell her I just need a wash, curl, and trim."

"Okay, I'll let her know." She hesitated before speaking again. "Donna, I know this is none of my business, but are you sure you want to come here? I mean, Sabrina is not your biggest fan right now."

I took a deep breath to give myself time to compose myself. "Good looking out, Jazzy, but I'm not coming there for Sabrina. I'm coming because my hair is a hot-ass mess and I can't get an appointment with Sheena. Trust me when I say that I am not thinking about Sabrina."

"Oh, well, umm." She was getting flustered. "Do me a favor and please don't mention what I said to anyone, okay?"

I laughed. "Don't worry, girl, I got your back. It'll stay between us."

"Thanks, Donna, and I'll see you at one."

Jasmine was such a sweet girl, and I hated that she had to be subjected to all of Sabrina's antics. I knew she only stuck around because she had to. She was a single mother who worked part-time at Sabrina's shop on top of being a full-time student. Thank God she would be graduating soon, because then she could leave behind all of the drama Sabrina and the salon provided.

I heard Keith in the shower when I hung up, so I made the bed and waited for my turn in the bathroom. Bored with waiting,

I got into the shower with Keith and passed the time doing all of the dirty things wet dreams are made of.

Driving to the salon, I sang along to the oldies but goodies that WDAS was playing. My day started off great, and I had plenty to smile about. It was a warm 75 degrees and the sun was shining bright, and, to top it off, I just had mind-blowing sex with the man I love. I hoped my day wouldn't be ruined by having a confrontation with Sabrina. My cell phone rang, interrupting my thoughts and, thinking it was Keith, I smiled and rushed to answer it.

Without looking at the display, I flipped it open and cooed, "Hey baby, you miss me already?"

"I can't remember the last time I was able to say that to somebody. It must be nice," Jackie said solemnly.

My smile vanished at the tone of her voice. "Hey girl, I'm sorry, I thought you were Keith. What's up? You sound like something's wrong."

I heard the unmistakable sound of Jackie crying. "What's wrong, Jackie? Did Jarrod hurt you again?"

I hadn't spoken to her since the last time I was over her house and she was considering letting that bastard back home.

She sniffed and tried to talk through her tears, "He did more than hurt me, he...he..."

I had to drive a few blocks before I was finally able to pull my car over and wait for her to calm down. I tried to reassure her that no matter what the problem was, it would be okay.

"No, it's not okay," she finally blurted out. "Jarrod is HIV positive, and Naomi and I might be too!" Once again, she began crying uncontrollably.

"What!" My day was officially ruined. My thoughts immediately went to Keith. This was my worst fear in dealing with a bisexual man, contracting a disease that I couldn't get rid of. Another thought crossed my mind. Sabrina. From what I'd been hearing, she and Jarrod had been getting hot and heavy for a while now. Regardless of our petty disagreements, I still cared about her.

"Yes, I found out a couple days ago," she sniffed.

"Oh my God, Jackie, I am so sorry to hear that. Are you okay?" My heart went out to her.

"No. I had to take Naomi down to the doctor's office so we could both be tested."

"Did you get your results?" I asked in shock.

"Not yet. I won't know until Monday." She put the phone down to blow her nose. "I hate that I had to call and tell you this, but I thought you would rather hear it from me than his doctor."

"Wh…what do you mean, hear it from his doctor? Hear what?" I stuttered.

"He asked me for the names of anyone Jarrod or I have had sex with because they need to be notified and tested. And I thought of Jarrod being with Keith and all, and I felt like I should be the one to tell you that you should get tested." She said her last words barely above a whisper.

I hesitated before responding, "Thank you for letting me know, Jackie, but Keith and I have already been tested." I appreciated Jackie's concern, but I felt confident that I was not at risk.

After finding out about Keith and Jarrod, I insisted that we both get tested. Even though he claimed he and Jarrod had never had intercourse, my first priority was my health, and I refused to have sex with him until well after we got our second round of STD tests. Another thing I had going in my favor was the fact that Keith and I had always used condoms.

"I'm glad one of us is confident about our status," she said through her tears.

"What did Jarrod have to say about it? Where is he?" I asked.

I felt guilty because I had begun thinking that she was stupid for sticking with Jarrod after the first time he hit her. Once she began talking about letting him come back home, I thought anybody who would stay and endure physical and emotional abuse deserved it. But this was something more. This was a death sentence.

"He's in jail," she said somberly.

"In jail? For what?" I asked in disbelief.

"It's a long story, and I don't feel like getting into it right now."

"Is there anything I can do for you?" I asked, not sure of what else to say.

"The only person who can help me is God, but thank you, anyway."

"Jackie, please call me and let me know what the doctor says, okay?"

"Okay, thank you."

"No, thank you for thinking enough of me to tell me personally. If you need anything, and I mean anything, I'm here for you."

"Bye, Donna." She hung up.

I sat in my car thinking of how I could have just as easily been in Jackie's shoes. Although Keith had firmly denied having any sexual contact with Jarrod since I caught the two of them together, I still held my doubts. After all, Jarrod had been going out of his way lately to cause trouble between us. I began to wonder what was really going on with him and Keith and if they still had unfinished business. But from what I could tell, Keith had been on his best behavior, so I pushed the negative thoughts out of my head and decided to give my man the benefit of the doubt. Besides, I made sure Keith wore condoms, so the chances of me contracting anything were slim. I put my car in gear to drive off, but a thought occurred to me that made me slam my foot on the brake. Thinking back to the night of my birthday when Keith and I stayed at the Four Seasons, I remembered that I let him cum in my mouth. What's worse was that I didn't spit it out. A feeling of nausea came over me, and I had to open the window to get some fresh air. It was several minutes before my hands stopped shaking and I was able to drive. My first plan of action when I returned home from the salon was to confront Keith with the news about Jarrod and make plans to get retested. I hoped for Keith's sake that this test came back negative, or else he would surely die a slow painful death, and it wouldn't be from the virus.

* * *

My walk of shame into the salon was worse than I could have imagined. It was surreal, like something out of a movie, where the music screeches to a halt and everything happens in slow motion.

"Hey, everybody," I called out as I walked to one of the few available seats.

Lena was busy eating a sandwich and when she saw me enter, she held up a finger signaling me to wait. I nodded my head and scanned the table for a magazine to read to keep me from noticing the whispers all around me.

There were a few people who seemed genuinely happy to see me, while others either stared in shock or mumbled their greetings. Sabrina, on the other hand, put down the curling iron she was holding and stepped forward.

"Look what the cat dragged in," she said snidely.

"Hello to you too, Sabrina," I said before burying my face into the year-old *Essence* magazine I was pretending to read.

"So, what brings you in here today? You slummin' or something?"

There were a few snickers from the onlookers. I refused to allow Sabrina to antagonize me, so I brushed off her comment.

"Not at all. I'm just trying to get my hair done."

Lena signaled for me to sit at the sink and I jumped up almost knocking over a table.

I closed my eyes while Lena washed my hair, and hoped that for once, Sabrina would act her age and let bygones be bygones. But, deep down, I knew that would never happen.

With the towel wrapped around my head, I walked to Lena's station and sat down. I looked up and saw Sabrina looking at me while whispering to her client, who was also staring at me, but with a shocked expression.

"So how have you been, Lena?" I was trying to make small talk to pass the time.

"I've been good. How about you?"

"Good, thanks." I was racking my brain for an interesting topic of discussion to discuss with her, when her cell phone rang.

She looked at the display and said apologetically, "I really have to take this. It's my mom, and she's watching my son for me today. He's been sick, so I need to make sure he's okay. I'll only be a minute."

"No problem, I hope everything is all right," I said, but she was already walking toward the back room to take the call.

I sat in the chair, feeling totally uncomfortable and wishing I knew how to do my own hair. I picked up another magazine and flipped through the pages.

"Listen up, everybody," Sabrina called out. "I have a blind item!" The ghetto Wendy Williams was at it again. Groans could be heard all around. Understandably so, because a few of Sabrina's previous "blind item" victims were present. Refusing to be a part of her bullying, I kept reading.

"Are ya'll ready for this? It's a good one. Donna!" I looked up and saw Sabrina looking at me with a conniving grin on her face. "I think you might appreciate this one."

I was getting uneasy, and somewhere deep in my belly, a knot was forming.

"What goody two-shoes' soon-to-be-husband likes a little dick on the side?"

What she'd said was so obvious, everyone turned to look at me. No one said a word as they all waited for the fireworks. My heart was beating so loud, I was sure everyone in the shop could hear it, and it took everything I had in me not to get up and choke the life out of Sabrina. I looked around and realized that everyone in the shop was waiting for me to either fight or respond. So, I chose the latter. I walked over to where Sabrina was standing and stood directly in front of her. She took a step forward and got in my face.

"What the fuck you gonna do?" she challenged with her fists balled at her sides.

I smiled deviously at her as a thought occurred to me.

Spinning around to face my audience, I called out, "I have a little blind item of my own, everybody." I turned back around to Sabrina, who wore a puzzled expression. "And I'm sure *you* would appreciate this one." I cleared my throat for emphasis. "What chickenhead hairdresser is sleeping with a *very* married down-low brotha who has recently tested positive for HIV?"

"Oh shit," somebody in the crowd screamed, as several other people began talking in loud whispers.

Satisfied with the crowd's reaction, I turned away from Sabrina's stunned expression and walked out the door. The ride home was bittersweet, because I was satisfied that I had, once and for all, shut Sabrina up. But I hated that our friendship had been reduced to airing each other's dirty laundry. And to top it all off, my hair was in worse condition than before. My day was beyond ruined, and all I could think of was getting home and hiding under the covers.

"Keith! Keith!" I called after slamming the front door behind me. I bent over at the waist to catch my breath.

"Hey, baby." He walked halfway down the stairs, took one look at my hair, and stopped. "What the hell? I thought you went to get your hair done?"

"Come down here. We need to talk." I signaled for him to follow me into the living room.

"Oh boy," he said as he plopped down on the couch. "What is it now?"

"I talked to Jackie today, and guess what she told me?"

He shrugged his shoulders. "What?"

I took a deep breath, "Jarrod tested positive for HIV."

His eyebrows shot up and his mouth dropped open. "Are you serious?" he whispered.

"Do I look like I'm playing?" I spat, with my arms crossed.

He held up his arms in defense. "Whoa, why are you mad at me? It's not my fault."

"I didn't say that, but hearing about Jarrod hit a little too close to home, if you know what I'm saying."

Keith's face was contorted in confusion, "Donna, are you saying you think I have it?"

I nervously shuffled my feet and remained quiet.

"Aww, come on, Donna. I thought we moved past this."

"Who said we moved past this?" I looked around the room. "I sure didn't. I may have forgiven you, but there is no way I can forget."

He reached over and pulled me down next to him on the couch. "Donna I need you to trust me. I don't have any diseases. Remember, you were there when I got my results." He reached around and began massaging my neck.

I moved out of his reach and said, "Keith, I need you to be totally honest with me. Have you and Jarrod been together since I saw the two of you together?"

"Absolutely not." I didn't realize I was holding my breath until I forcibly exhaled.

I looked at him skeptically. I wanted to believe him, but I needed reassurance.

"So why has he been popping up so much lately? And what he did to you at the fundraiser reminded me of a scorned lover."

I searched his face for any sign of deceit, but he showed nothing.

He shrugged his shoulders. "Jarrod is a sick individual, no pun intended, and I guess he was trying to get me back for telling Jackie about us."

"Well, there's only one thing left to do. We have to get tested again."

"That's not a problem. I am a hundred percent confident that I am clean."

"You better not be lying to me, Keith."

He held up three fingers. "Scout's honor."

He wrapped his arms around me and pulled me into a hug. I laid my head on his chest and listened to the melodic sound of his beating heart. He ran his fingers through the ends of my hair.

"So, are you going to tell me what happened with your hair?"

"I had to go to Sabrina's salon to get my hair done, and to make a long story short, she told everybody in the shop that you're gay."

It was his turn to push me away. "What?"

I nodded my head and said, "Yup. Then I told her and everybody else that she was sleeping with a man who has HIV."

He jumped up and stood over top of me. "That dirty mother-fucker! I don't believe he told her that. And to think, I actually felt sorry for him. I don't believe this shit."

I pulled my knees to my chest and watched as Keith frantically paced the floor.

"He's out here spreading diseases, and yet he still finds ways to try and ruin my life."

"Yeah, and Jackie is understandably distraught, because she doesn't know if she has it yet. And I don't even want to think about the poor baby, who's an innocent victim in all of this." I cringed at the thought of little Naomi having to take medication for the rest of her life.

Suddenly, Keith stopped in his tracks and slumped down into the nearest chair. His face was pale, and he began trembling.

I hurried over to his side and knelt down. "Keith, what's wrong?" My first thought was that he was going to admit to sleeping with Jarrod.

"My father...my father is sleeping with Ms. Elaine, the pastor's wife."

"I know, you told me. So why are you so upset now?"

I was able to put two and two together before he could answer. Since Mr. Reed and Ms. Elaine were having an affair, and Jarrod and Pastor Douglas were sleeping together, it was possible his father could have been exposed.

"Oh, my God, Keith. You think your father may have it?" I took hold of his hands.

"When it rains it pours, doesn't it?" He looked at me, and I could have sworn I saw tears in his eyes.

"Are you going to tell him?" I asked.

He exhaled loudly. "That's if he'll even listen to me. I haven't talked to him since the fundraiser. But I was thinking of going down to the office this week to talk to him."

"Do you want me to go with you?"

He shook his head. "No, I'll be all right. I have to face his sooner or later, and after hearing this mess about Jarrod, it's going to have to be sooner than later."

"It's going to be okay, baby. You know I have your back."

He chuckled. "I know, and thank you."

I stood up and looked in the mirror. "Ugh, I look a hot mess," I said while running my fingers through my now dry and frizzy hair.

Keith didn't respond. He stared off into space and never looked my way. I kissed him on top of his head and walked upstairs to try to work a miracle on my head.

KEITH

Donna took an early lunch on Monday so we could go and get retested. We found a clinic in Center City that offered the rapid HIV test, and one hour later, we had our results.

"See, I told you," I teased. I held up my results and waved it in front of her face.

"Yeah, yeah, yeah," she laughed. "Lucky for you."

"Come on, Donna, are you going to trust me now?"

"Only as much as you allow me to," she said when we reached her car.

I opened the door for her to let her in. I waited while she started the car and rolled down her window.

"So what are you about to do?" she asked.

"I think I'm going to go over to the office, because it's time to face the music."

"Are you going to tell you father about Jarrod?"

"I think so." I smiled at her. "I don't even want to think about it right now."

"If you say so, but if you need me, call me, okay."

I leaned in the window and kissed her softly. "Have I told you lately how much I love you?"

"You just did." She waved goodbye and pulled out of the parking lot.

When I arrived at the office, I was relieved to see that it was empty. I walked into my office and shut the door behind me for some privacy. It took about an hour for me to get through a week's worth of email and voicemail messages. As I expected, most of the messages were from members of the league offering support. The last message, however, took me by surprise. It was from Corey. He said he was back in D.C. and he asked me to call him. Before he hung up, he told me that he would understand if I chose not to help him with the new chapter, but he would really like to hear from me. I decided at that moment to leave the past in the past and placed the phone back in its cradle.

Outside of my office door, I heard my father and Mrs. Knickson talking in hushed tones. I walked around my desk and listened at the door. From what I could gather, Mrs. Knickson was alarmed that my door was shut, because when she left, the door was open. My father, on the other hand, wasn't concerned, he was trying to coax Mrs. Knickson back to his office. Before she relented and followed him, I snatched the door open.

Mrs. Knickson looked ready to faint, and my father's face changed from surprise to contempt.

"You have some nerve showing your face down here!" he yelled.

Mrs. Knickson looked from me to my father and quickly excused herself.

"Dad, can we talk in private?" I asked in a muted voice.

"Don't call me 'Dad.' My son is dead!"

I would have rather he spit in my face than say those words to me.

"Dad, please."

"Please what? Do you have any idea the kind of damage you have done to my reputation? Not to mention the business we stand to lose because of the *lifestyle* you have chosen."

"I haven't *chosen* anything, and none of our clients care about what goes on in the privacy of my bedroom."

He waved me away. "You're not welcome here anymore. As a matter of fact, it's good that you came in today, because it saves me the trouble of packing your shit and throwing it out on the trash." He turned to walk away. "I expect you to be gone by the close of business today," he called over his shoulder.

I knew seeing him would not be a pleasant experience but I had no idea it would turn this ugly. Resisting the urge to throw in the towel and walk out of my father's life forever, I jogged down the hall to catch up with him.

"Would you stop acting like a child and listen?" I yelled when I reached his office.

"Nothing you have to say is worth listening to. Here I thought I raised a man and you turn out to be some queer who's only pretending to be a man! I knew I should have taken the reigns from your mother. I told her she was raising a wimp, and look what happened. I can't believe it, my *son*, a fucking *faggot*!" he spat.

I opened my mouth to defend myself, but he silenced me

with his hand. From the corner of my eye, I could see Mrs. Knickson pretending to busy herself.

"And to think, all of the women you ran around with, and now engaged to be married to a whore. I guess the two if you go good together, both of you like men. Get out of my face!"

The mention of Donna brought up the information she shared with me. "Oh, so she's a whore now? Well, she wasn't too much of a whore for you to come on to her, was she?" I stepped further in his office. "Yeah, she told me exactly what you said to her. You have some nerve calling her names and playing high and mighty when you are the biggest whore out here. Did you actually think she would leave me to be with you, *old man*?"

"And so what if I did step on your toes? She needs a real man, anyway. What can you do for her? Bring another man into the bedroom and let her watch, you queen! Now, for the last time, leave my office. I don't need you here anymore. I have no use for you. Consider yourself dismissed." He pointed his finger at the door as he stomped toward me.

"You know what? Fuck you, *Dad*. I'm going to leave, but you best believe it won't be easy for you. You're going to have to buy me out. Don't forget, half of those properties belong to me, and I also have money invested in this business. And you can forget all of the contacts I have acquired, because they are coming with me. I don't need this shit from you. Take this business and shove it up your ass."

Mrs. Knickson must have sensed my father's next move, because she rushed over and stepped in between the two of us. My father pushed her out of the way and got in my face.

"No, Keith, shoving things up asses is your thing, not mine." He grunted loudly. "God only knows what kind of diseases you've picked up along the way."

Tired of his berating, I decided to go in for the kill. "Speaking of diseases, Dad, you need to think about getting yourself checked out. You see, instead of throwing my business in my face, you should have been paying more attention to who you were fucking. I found out that Jarrod tested positive for HIV."

"What the hell are you talking about? I don't have anything to do with that!" he growled.

"Oh, but you do, Dad. While you were putting your *thang* down with Ms. Elaine, Pastor Douglas was busy taking it up the ass from Jarrod. Do you see where this is going? Does it have anything to do with you yet, Dad? How does the saying go, what goes around, comes around? Everything comes full circle, Dad. Remember that!"

With that, I spun on my heels and walked out of his office, leaving him standing there with his mouth hanging open. Mrs. Knickson, who'd witnessed the entire exchange, darted to the nearest wastebasket and emptied the contents of her stomach. I shook my head at her in disgust. In my eyes, she was just as guilty as my father, because she jeopardized her husband's life, all for a good time with my father.

Once in my soon-to-be-former office, I threw all of my personal belongings in a trash bag and gathered anything that would be useful to me in opening my own office. I dragged the bags down the hall and into the elevator. The door to my father's office was closed, but I heard Mrs. Knickson screaming at the top her lungs threatening to kill my father. My first reaction was to walk in and attempt to calm her down, but I elected to mind my own business. My first priority was to begin the dissolution of my interest in my father's business and make a fresh start on my own. The drive home was surprisingly peaceful, despite the altercation with my father. For a long time I hid my true self from everyone, namely my father, for fear of being ostracized. But now that it was out in the open, it felt good not having that cloud of secrecy hanging over my head. I finally felt free. After all, my woman chose to stay with me regardless of my past, and I no longer carried the burden of my secret. Life was good.

JACKIE
AND
JARROD

Jackie entered Carrabba's Italian Grill and scanned the room for Sean. She spotted him and walked to the table where he was seated. His back was to her, so he didn't notice her until she put her hands over his eyes and said, "Guess who?"

Sean grabbed her wrists and said, "I bet it's the prettiest girl in the room."

Jackie giggled as he stood up and gave her big hug.

"How are you?" she asked.

"I'm great now that you're here." He pulled out her chair and waited for her to be seated before sitting back down.

Jackie looked across the table at Sean and once again admired his good looks. Since arresting Jarrod, Sean had become a great friend to her. He made no secret of the fact that he was interested in being more than just friends, but Jackie kept him at arm's length. She was flattered by his attention, but she knew it would take some time before she could heal properly from the emotional abuse she'd endured from Jarrod. So in the meantime, Sean planned to be there for her in any way she needed him, because he knew a good thing when he saw it, and in his eyes Jackie was the real thing.

Jackie couldn't believe how much she grew to like Sean in such a short time. She began to open up to him in ways that surprised her, even going as far as to tell him about Jarrod's diagnosis. During one of their lengthy telephone conversations, Jackie began crying when Sean mentioned having a brother who contracted the AIDS virus and died. Sean tried to console Jackie, thinking he said something wrong. When she finally composed herself, Jackie shared the story of her HIV scare, starting with the phone call from Jarrod's doctor, to her and Naomi's subsequent tests and results. Sean was in a state of shock from Jackie's story and initially thought her outburst meant she and the baby also tested positive. To his great relief, Jackie informed him that she and Naomi both tested negative. She explained that she was crying because of how close she came to possibly losing her life as a result of someone else's actions.

For a few days after that, Jackie began distancing herself from Sean and he couldn't understand why. So he was obviously pleased when Jackie called him the day before and invited him to dinner. He didn't ask why, because he really didn't care, and he really wanted to see her again.

"It's good to see you again, Jackie. You look great." His million-dollar smile tugged at her heart.

Jackie blushed and ran her hands over her clothes.

"I guess I look better than the last time you saw me, huh?"

Sean reached across the table to take hold of her hand. "You were beautiful even then."

Jackie found herself getting lost in his eyes, and she had to look away as she began thinking of how long it had been since she'd had sex.

"I was happy when you called and invited me out, and, I must say, a little surprised too," Sean said.

Jackie nodded her head and smiled. "I know. I kind of surprised myself. But I needed to get out of that house, *and* I wanted to thank you by treating you to dinner, so I figured I would kill two birds with one stone."

"Good thinking." He hesitated. "So, have you talked to your husband?"

"Nope. I have nothing to say to him. The last I heard, his mother told me he couldn't make bail, and he was threatening to put the house up for money."

"Can he do that?"

"Not if I don't sign on the dotted line. And after what he put me through, he'll never see the light of day, if I have any say so."

"I hate to bring this up, but did the doctor say anything about getting retested? I know they say that if you've been exposed to the virus, you should get tested every six months." Sean hoped he didn't ruin the evening by asking that question. But to his delight, Jackie remained upbeat.

"Yeah, when I got my results, the doctor recommended Naomi and I get tested again. But he also said that Jarrod could have contracted the virus while I was pregnant." Sean grimaced.

Jackie knew what he was thinking and smiled. "No, that's a good thing. Lucky for me, no matter how hard I tried, Jarrod refused to make love to me once he found out I was pregnant. So, you see, that's why I'm pretty confident that we'll be okay."

Sean breathed a sigh of relief. It wasn't that he would desert Jackie if she tested positive, but he wasn't sure he would be able to handle a relationship knowing that she was sick.

The waitress came and took their orders, and they spent the rest of the evening getting to know each other better as friends. Sean was a refreshing change from Jarrod, and he was able to make Jackie laugh for the first time in months. When they said their goodbyes, Sean asked her to let him return the favor by allowing him to treat her to a movie the following weekend. Jackie surprised herself by saying yes and promising to call him the next day.

When Jackie returned home from her evening with Sean, she felt refreshed. Ms. James, who was sitting in the kitchen making faces at Naomi, called out to her when she heard her enter.

"Did you enjoy yourself?" she asked with a knowing look.

Jackie leaned over and kissed Ms. James on the cheek and Naomi on her head.

"I did, and thank you so much for watching the baby for me. I really needed to get out and clear my head."

"Well, you certainly look clear to me," Ms. James laughed.

Jackie was on cloud nine and it was painfully obvious to Ms. James that she was falling for her new "friend."

"Jackie, I'm happy that you're happy, but I don't want you to move too fast with this guy."

She hated to burst Jackie's bubble, but she didn't want anyone to take advantage of her daughter-in-law while she was still so vulnerable.

Jackie's smile disappeared from her face. "I'm not moving fast. He's just a friend."

Ms. James cocked her head to the side and looked at Jackie disapprovingly.

"Okay. So what if I like him? He's a nice guy and easy to talk to. Besides, with Jarrod gone, I'm going to have to move on with my life at some point in time."

Ms. James placed Naomi in her seat and walked over to Jackie. "I'm not saying you shouldn't move on, baby. Just take it slow. Whether you know it or not, you are still scarred from your relationship with my son and it's going to affect this relationship if you don't give yourself time to heal."

Jackie attempted to blink away the tears that began forming in her eyes, and Ms. James pulled her into a hug.

"If you really like this man you need to be fair to him and learn to be happy with yourself." Ms. James held Jackie's face in her hands and wiped her eyes. "More importantly, sweetie, you have to be fair to yourself. You are not ready to jump into a relationship, no matter how horny you are." They both cracked up laughing and hugged tightly.

"Thank you," Jackie said.

"No, thank you for not shutting me out of your lives because of my son's behavior."

"I would never do that. You've been like a mother to me, and I love you for it."

"Speaking of my son, you need to think about starting the divorce proceedings. There's no need to drag this out. Cut your ties as soon as possible," Ms. James said.

"I planned on contacting a lawyer as soon as I figured out how much money I would need."

"Don't worry about money. I'll pay for it if necessary. I can refer you to a couple of good lawyers if you like. I can call in a few favors and maybe even get it done pro bono."

"I had planned on calling Keith's fiancé, Donna, because she works for a lawyer, but if you know someone, then that's even better."

After putting Naomi to bed, Ms. James had Jackie gather all of Jarrod's financial statements so she could get a better understanding of her financial situation. Jackie learned that Jarrod kept large sums of money hidden in bank accounts that she was not aware of. By the end of the night, Jackie felt much more confident that she would be financially set and would even be able to stay home with Naomi for as long as she wanted. Things were certainly looking up for her, and for the first time in a while, she was at peace.

DONNA

"So what did you think of that place?" I asked Keith as he navigated his way through rush-hour traffic.

"I think it's perfect. The location is perfect and the office space is perfect. Let's just hope the price is perfect," he said.

We were on our way back from seeing yet another office for Keith to move into. Lately, our days consisted of Keith scouting the city for potential sites and me calling for prices and availability. After seeing how hard Keith was working to branch out on his own, I decided to use my remaining vacation time to help ease his transition. The last property we looked at was in the heart of University City and was a prime location for Keith to expand his business. From the look on his face when we entered the building, I knew he was in love. The only problem would be the rent for the location. His main concern was paying rent as well as paying to employ an office manager.

"So do you have any ideas about who you want as an office manager?" I asked.

"Yes and no. Curt, who's the secretary of the league, told me his wife is thinking of retiring, and will probably be looking for a part-time job in the next few months. The only problem is money. I can't expect her to work for nothing, and I can't pay her a ton of money either."

"How much do you think you can afford?"

"No more than nine or ten bucks an hour, at least until I get myself on my feet."

I reached over and massaged his neck. "It'll be okay, baby. Is there anything I can do to help?"

"Just keep doing what you're doing. You standing by me means the world to me."

I smiled and continued to rub his neck. When Keith walked away from the business he shared with his father, things began to get tight. He explained to me that while we wouldn't be broke, we would definitely need to cut back on expenses. Even with the money he stood to gain by his father's buying him out, it would still take some time before his financial situation was back to normal. When he shared the office space with his father, they split the cost of expenses, such as rent and staff wages. But now that he was on his own, he had to foot the bill by himself. Seeing how stressed he was becoming, I offered to push our wedding back until in order to save some money. He was extremely grateful and, in return, promised me the wedding of my dreams and a two-week honeymoon. I thought it was more than fair, so I agreed.

Keith went straight to our bedroom when we got home, and I went to the kitchen to start dinner.

I was beginning to enjoy being home from work so much that I had become a real Susie Homemaker. The house was immaculate, and I cooked breakfast and dinner every day. I turned on the stereo and danced to "Candy," by Cameo, while making the salad. I was dropping it like it's hot when the doorbell rang. I threw down the dishtowel and danced over to the front door.

When I opened the door, my face fell, and I frowned.

"Well, well, well, look what the cat dragged in," I said, hand on hip.

Sabrina stood in the doorway and said nothing. I went to turn the stereo off, and, when I returned, she hadn't moved. This was the first time I had seen or talked to her since the incident at her shop, and I wondered why she decided to show her face today. I took a good look at her and noticed that she looked a mess. Her hair was matted to her head, and she looked like she lost about ten pounds. I put all of my anger at her aside and led her into the house before closing the door behind her. She fell into my arms and wept. I held her up as I guided her to the couch.

"What's wrong, Sabrina. Why are you crying?" I asked softly.

She tried speaking, but only managed jumbled words.

"Is there something wrong with one of your sisters?" I was getting worried.

She shook her head violently and curled herself into a ball on the couch.

Keith came down the steps to see what the commotion was. He looked at Sabrina, and I shrugged my shoulders. I got up and gestured for him to follow me into the kitchen.

"What the hell is she doing here, and why is she snottin' on my furniture?" he hissed angrily.

"I don't know, Keith. She just showed up at the door and started crying. I'm trying to figure out what's going on."

"After the shit she did to you, and to us, why do you care?"

"Because she's my friend," I whispered.

"No, she *was* your friend. So, either you get her out of here, or I will." He crossed his arms defensively.

"All right, Keith, I will. But first I need to find out what's going on." He opened his mouth to protest, but I put my hand up and silenced him. "Don't start, Keith. Do I need to remind you that I put up with Jarrod longer than necessary?"

He looked away and put his hands in the air. "Fine, do what you have to do, but I don't want her in here when I come down for dinner."

He turned away from me and stomped back up the stairs.

I poured two glasses of juice and carried them into the living room. Sabrina had her face buried in the pillow to muffle the sounds of her cries. I sat her up and wiped her face.

"Talk to me, Sabrina," I said softly.

She remained silent.

"Look you can't just show up crying on my doorstep after all that has happened and not tell me what's going on."

Her head dropped to her chest. "I'm sorry," she whimpered.

"What was that?" I couldn't help myself. It was so rare that she would ever utter those words that I had to hear them again.

She sighed deeply. "I said, I'm sorry."

"Okay. I know that's not what you came here to tell me. So what's going on?"

"After you told me about Jarrod, I went and got tested." She began to sob.

It all made sense. "Oh, my God, Sabrina. I am so sorry." I wrapped my arms around her tightly.

She pulled away from me. "I found out a few days ago. I finally got up enough nerve to get tested, and I got my results yesterday."

"Have you talked to Jarrod?" I asked.

She nodded. "The day after you told me, he called me from jail. He said his wife got him locked up on some bogus charges, and he was trying to get me to beat her up." She wiped her nose on the back of her hand. "You know what? I was so sprung over that mother-fucker that I was going to do it. I was actually going to go over to his house and beat his wife's ass. Can you believe it?"

The sad part was that I *could* believe it.

"But," she continued, "something told me to ask him about, you know, what you said. I didn't really believe you, but I thought I would ask him, and we would get a good laugh about it. Anyway, when I asked him about it, he flipped out. He started calling me names and told me I was the one who gave it to him. I couldn't believe it, and then he hung up on me. I haven't heard from him since."

I didn't know what to say. My first thought was to tell her, "I told you so," but I didn't want to go there.

"Are you going to be okay?" It was the only thing I could think of, and, after I said it, I realized how stupid it sounded.

"No, I'm not okay, and I don't think I will ever be. The worst part of it all is that I really can't blame Jarrod," she murmured.

"What do you mean?" I asked.

"I mean, I can't be sure that I even got it from him or not. All of this time, I was out there thinking that I was invincible and shit, I wasn't using any rubbers."

"Oh, Sabrina," I sighed.

She leaned into me for a hug and wept. For the next hour, we talked and cried. Seeing her like this made me appreciate everything I had and let me know how easy it would have been for me to be in her position. After we were all cried out, I walked her to the door and said goodbye, and told her that no matter what, I would be there for her.

"Donna," she said before leaving, "please forgive me. I am so sorry for everything. And please tell Keith I'm sorry. I love you."

I hugged her once more and said, "I love you too."

The first day of summer was also my last day of work. I decided to quit my job and work as Keith's office manager. After thinking it over, I approached him with the idea of my working for him.

"Are you for real?" he asked with a surprised look on his face.

"Of course I am. Look at it this way, if you hire me, you can save money, because you don't have to pay me. And, since

I'm going to be your wife, I think it's time I learned the business. Don't you agree?"

"Do I!" He picked me up and spun me around.

Six weeks later, KDR Holdings, LLC, was open for business. Once again, all was well in Paradise.

EPILOGUE
One Year Later

Keith and Donna exchanged vows at sunset on a beach in Paradise Island, Bahamas. Jackie attended with her new best friend and lover, Sean, and Naomi, who had just begun to walk, was the cutest flower girl ever. As he promised, Keith gave Donna a two-week honeymoon. Keith thought life couldn't get any better, until Donna gave him a surprise of her own. She handed him a small gift-wrapped box that contained a positive pregnancy test. Keith was ecstatic, because his family was finally complete.

Mr. Reed did test positive for HIV, as did Pastor Douglas and Ms. Elaine. Mr. Reed continued living the life of a bachelor, finding a whole new batch of women to keep him occupied. Pastor Douglas and Ms. Elaine left the church in shame after their secret lives were discovered by the clergy. Mrs. Knickson's life was spared. She tested negative for the virus and quit her job with Mr. Reed, and her husband was none the wiser.

Sabrina did not keep in contact with Donna. Sabrina contacted several of the men she'd slept with to tell them her diagnosis, and, after receiving numerous death threats, she moved to Atlanta to live with family members.

Jarrod was finally released on bail, to house arrest. While awaiting trial, he was notified by the New Jersey Bar that his license to practice law had been revoked. He is currently serving his house arrest in his mother's basement.

Author Bio

Brooke Green is a manager at a large telecommunications company, and currently resides in Philadelphia, PA with her 2 daughters. She is hard at work on her next book, but would love to hear your feedback on *You, Me, and He* at Brookegreen76@aol.com or www.myspace.com/malikasimone

Full Circle Publishing

Name: _____

Address: _____

City/State: _____

Zip: _____

$14.95/Book

Quantity	TOTAL
Shipping/Handling	**FREE**

TOTAL $_____

To order online visit
www.fullcirclepub.com

Send check or money order to:
P.O. Box 16868 • Philadelphia, PA 19142